T0161194

In *Tiny*, Mairead Case crawls inside pain to open a door into the sky—only the stars may be able to provide a map for how to stay present in grief without always mourning. While permanent war forms the backdrop of this novel, intimate connection between friends, lovers, strangers, and accomplices offers a way to imagine survival in a world predicated on death. This is a book that expertly conjures the hopes of a teenage imagination not yet destroyed, searching for ways to express the intensity of every single emotion so that no one has to give up just in order to go on.

—Mattilda Bernstein Sycamore

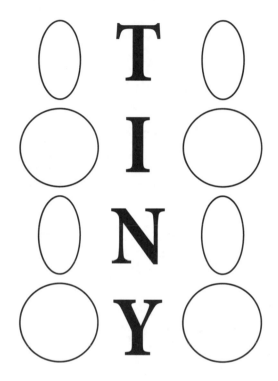

TINY

MAIREAD CASE

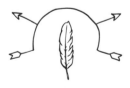

*fe*atherproof BOOKS

Excerpts published in: *ENTROPY, What Are Birds?,* and *Maggot Brain*. Thank you to editors Janice Lee, Shay Reynolds, Bennett Nieberg, and Mike McGonigal.

Published by
*feather*proof books
Chicago, Illinois
www.featherproof.com

First edition
10 9 8 7 6 5 4 3 2 1

Library of Congress Control Number: 2020943825
ISBN 13: 9781943888221

Edited by Sammi Skolmoski
Design by Zach Dodson
Proofread by Sam Axelrod
Author photo by Drew Bouchard

Printed in the United States of America
Set in Minion

for Maggie Queeney

It matters what stories we tell to tell other stories with; it matters what concepts we think to think other concepts with.

—Donna Haraway

Often I remember that you likewise have been denied the relief and pleasure of stillness. When I do, my heart breaks. When it does, I gather the shards into the shape of a country, then I close my eyes and swallow.

—Billy-Ray Belcourt

This is for forever: the only time I believed it.

—Tracy + the Plastics

PEOPLE & BIRDS

TINY *is here.*

IZZY, *Tiny's sister and oldest friend, lives next door.*
HANK *is Tiny's boyfriend, and*
KELLEY *is Tiny's brother.*

BEAR *is Tiny and Kelley's dad.*
TINY'S MOTHER *studies hearts.*

AUNT CHARLOTTE *is Tiny's mother's friend.*
She is also a painter.

MERYL *is Kelley's girlfriend.*

THUY, MARNIE & SHAWN *organize UP IN ARMS, a*
dance party.

Also, lots of CROWS: American, hooded, carrion, with
purple-black feathers.

PLACE

By the water, in a city full of moss and blown-out pearly light.

REMEMBER

Some of these people are dead, and some are alive. Some are
in-between. Sometimes, it changes. Tiny hears her mother's
voice frequently, especially in early mornings and otherwise-
empty rooms. Sometimes, coming out of hazy pain, Tiny can
point at the voice or it halos her.

Say it: here we are. Now is the time.

There are always multiple times and possibilities. The work is to stay with them.

It is dark. Tiny sits on the roof with her hand in front of her face. She can't see her hand, which is also her mother's hand. Their nails are painted green. Green for money, for growth without pain, even though Tiny doesn't really mind being hurt. She knows it's temporary, like the cold right after jumping into a lake, and even when the pain is everywhere. But every color stands for something, whether people understand it the same way or not, and that is comforting. It connects. Tiny painted her nails herself. She runs her palms up and down her thighs, to warm them and brush away wet grass.

It is windy, and though Tiny can't see that either, she can see the slick flickering over everything and hear the wind in the maples. This city is always raining, or between rain, except for two weeks in August when everything is a clear, firm-edged blue. Every few years, July is like that too, and then everyone talks about it. About how remarkable that is. It is remarkable for everyone to feel the same sun on the same day. Everyone has the same warmth on their faces. On other days, the light in Tiny's city bathes everything in vinegar, like it's a print ready to be soaked and rewound. People who think talking about the weather is boring have never had to be out in it together.

Tiny slides her right hand into her shirt so that she can feel the bones in her chest. She cups the tissue and slides her thumb across the place where ribs branch from her sternum. If Tiny's breast was a clock, her thumb would mark ten o'clock to midnight, again and again. Sometimes her thumb cramps. This is one kind of thinking. Tiny thinks about the soldiers who cut off their breasts so they could shoot arrows more accurately. In this way, they would always be soldiers. It might be like being a parent. Both situations are also physical facts that affect a person's ability to feed and eat, to work and travel. They affect how we are in the world, irreversibly. Where is the soft dent in your stomach. Why is that red line on your chest.

Tiny thinks this way when she misses her mother, who died when Tiny was a toddler. In science, Tiny read that babies are born with three hundred bones in their bodies, only those bones don't start growing until the second trimester. So when Tiny's chest formed, she was closer to being her mother than not. Babies are parasites first. Tiny used to be a blob. She remembers freckles on her mother's arms, but Tiny isn't sure if she remembers them from photos or actually being held. This city is too cold and gray for freckles. Tiny's mother lived in another place when she was little. Before Tiny was born, after it, and even now in death, Tiny's mother tells her daughter that she is a brilliant and strong person, resourceful and capable of absolutely everything life presents her. Tiny is a helper, not a fool, and that is a fact written in stars. Stars exist, even when people can't see them. Sometimes, planes are mistaken for stars, but stars exist. Stars exist.

Tiny thought she couldn't open the door, but she did.

Now she is thinking about nothing, and her mother, because Kelley is dead now too.

That's it.

That's the story.

Tiny thinks it, again and again, in and out of her body in time on the wet, windy roof.

Tiny knows her life is different now. Again.

For as long as she can remember, Tiny has felt pulled away from this house. It isn't a strong pull, but it is undeniable, like her third eye is also a metal, and magnets hover in the air outside. This is not a question of fate or forces, or even restlessness. It's a small headache, and a question about belonging. Tiny's home does not exist yet, or else it exists multiply, and in either case she must leave here to find it.

This is a fact. It is not something to fix.

When Tiny stands in front of something, she faces it.

Tiny is the tree growing towards the light and holding the dark. She is the plant growing on that tree, sponging food and water from the surrounding air, and she is the parasite eating the tree itself.

Something here will kill her too, but never, ever completely.

Tiny looked, looks, will look at death for so long that she isn't afraid of it anymore. She stared at death so long it could have opened its eyes back, suddenly in the dark. It could have made everything that wasn't Tiny into darkness too, like a girl waking up inside a whale in the ocean. But it didn't. And so, at first in a rushed lurch and then normal, as always, Tiny lives.

This is a responsibility. She takes it very seriously.

When living feels impossible, Tiny looks at the pictures of sheep, orchids, bees, lemurs, jellyfish, coral reefs, seals, moss, and microbes she drew inside of her mother's lab notebook in watercolor pencil. Tiny presses her hands into roofs, chair cushions, and the earth. She spreads out her fingers and pushes them flat, like she's about to arc into a handstand. A rainbow. Tiny drinks water and imagines her lungs full of color. She breathes out, imagining that color filling the room.

Because Tiny is responsible and holds memories, she exists and belongs. Because she is no longer afraid of that pain or contradiction, she will threaten people, or else they will treat her like a child. To them, Tiny will be a paradox of green fingernails, botanical faith, and buoyant heart. She will remind herself not to always apologize, or explain herself, or rationalize. We do not need to apologize for existing.

Tiny has never seen a coral reef in person, but she knows they exist. They are nests, apartments, museums, public housing, fields, individuals, and populations all at once. Their tones depend on sun, chemicals, creatures, and who's looking. They are, in as many ways as music can fill a room and the bodies inside it.

Izzy looks out her window, which faces the side of Tiny's house. On the ground in-between is glowing green lawn and cracked cement, dotted with periwinkles. There is no gate. When Tiny was little she could stand on this path with her arms out like wings and not touch either place.

Izzy can't really see Tiny, but she knows she's there because the roof looks like it has a hole. Everything is shiny from rain except the place where Tiny sits, mute in her black sweatshirt with the bandaged hands printed on it. Izzy remembers the summer Hank, Tiny's boyfriend, kept asking them to smoke with him. Yes, Tiny wanted to hold orange light in her mouth, a little fire in her hand. Quick treats make you easy to find.

Izzy found pictures of lungs like burnt marshmallows. She showed them to Tiny, but that rhetoric didn't work. Tiny already knew smoking was bad. She also knew death was inevitable. It was already her ghost. Later that summer, Tiny read an article about how smoking companies market to people in weak or vulnerable moments, and that's when she asked Hank to cut it out. Tiny would be fine just smelling the smoke in his hair. Izzy was mostly fine with that decision too. She knows her sister is not a fire to tend.

Tiny and Izzy are not sisters by blood, but they are sisters by everything else. Their mothers shared dress-up clothes, recipes, affordable travel tips, and escape plans. Their plans were usually elaborate, rarely unrealistic. Sometimes people think Tiny and Izzy are girlfriends. They let them think that. It's whatever. If people ask, however, Izzy and Tiny say intimacy isn't only for monogamous sexual relationships. They don't want to be poseurs. They promise to love each other always, and differently when necessary, like wave sets.

Three minutes later, a car sloshes down the street. The sound curves over wet leaves, and red taillights spark the puddles. The rain makes city air shine like a wiped-down mirror, and both sisters take that gleam into their lungs. Izzy is happy to know she and Tiny are home together. Waiting for Tiny to come back can be a constant, anxious swallowing that Izzy is learning to stop. Tiny doesn't want to be tracked. There is no other option. They've both tried. Both sisters see the car. It is a dark color, with six bumper stickers on the back. Izzy thinks one says EARTH. This is comforting. A goodnight. They don't have to say anything else to each other.

Tiny doesn't want to understand anything completely, ever, including herself. She would rather wonder a little bit. Or wander. This is like wishing to live forever.

People want to understand, and because of that some of them have a hard time not killing everything. Sometimes it's by accident. Sometimes it's necessary or for preservation. But to completely understand something, it must never change. There must be a null set, and so people explode mountains. They slice open chests. They name land separately from what it does, or did, or is, and especially when it never needed to be different in the first place.

But how do you look at a body and say:
when she was little, she wanted to be a fire truck?

How do you say love horrified them too?

How do we see home? How do you?

Desire changes like rings on a tree.

Sometimes different times and states are true at once. Sometimes people don't want to show everything, or they can't because they are wrestling it. Or wondering about it. Or laughing or sidetracked or blinded. Sometimes there aren't words.

When Tiny thinks about all of this, she feels old and young at once, and a cluster of white lights in her wrists and chest, humming.

When she was alive, Tiny's mother knew everything anyone could about hearts. She performed surgery on them and studied their rhythms. She traveled, and she asked questions. In one small room with plastic yellow light, Tiny's mother looked at thousands of frozen slices of heart, and then labeled and dyed them by herself. She taught Tiny how a cardiograph is actually a map of the heart moving to escape the body, then back into it. If that line kept moving, Tiny's mother said, your heart would burst out of your chest. Tiny used to imagine this whenever she sat down to eat with new people. *Plop!* Your heart's in the noodles. Hearts are brown, or yellow and brown, depending on the amount of blood and fat. Tiny knows this fact but still imagines them as pink and red, slick and mysterious. The ability to hold both truths is a strength, like seeing a cell phone tower at sunset and thinking it could be a ghost-chandelier instead. It could be.

By now, scientists can see and name every single part of a heart, but sometimes the muscle still surprises them. This is also true for brains, which aren't muscles even though people talk about exercising them. And it is true for death, which happens, and still people know very few absolutely sure things about it. Sometimes that truth is a scary movie, to Tiny, and sometimes it is warmth in her chest. It exists outside of her, and it doesn't. Tiny used to read, obsessively, about all the bad things that can happen to a heart. Hearts can die in

rhhhhhhhrz rhhhhhhhrz rhhhhhh

MAIREAD CASE   25

sections, they can swell, they can beat like this: *rhhhhhhhrz rhhhhhhhrz rhhhhhhhrz*. For Tiny, imagining this sound is like hearing that car on wet maple leaves. It is urgent, but not frightening. It is the way home.

rhhhhhhhrz rhhhhhhhrz rhhhhhh

Once, Tiny went to a birthday party, and the horror of mourning lowered around her head like a hood. She hadn't expected it. It blocked out the streamer colors and all of the sound.

After that, Tiny and Izzy promised each other to always be REAL PEOPLE, even when their teeth get soft or when they have too much money or too little. Even when they are distracted and need more time. Even when they are the adults, they will always work to change and break open and mourn and love. To remember when they need to and forget when they don't. It is important to try, and fail, and try differently.

As if Tiny could ever forget her mother. She can just look at her hands. It is almost a religion. This promise is both hopeless and hopeful, which is why it is so strong too. Her voice is in her head. All of them.

Once, in a magazine, Tiny read: You were given a life. What did you make of it?

It made her think about gifts she received and loved.
None of those gifts were people.

Sometimes Tiny has a bad feeling.
She doesn't have words for it.

Maybe it isn't actually bad, or even a feeling.

It rests at the top of her stomach, tucked underneath her ribs.
Tiny imagines opening her ribcage like the hood of a car and pulling the feeling out.

Look, she'd say. I can hold this. That means it isn't me.

Tiny has a recurring dream with a train station in it. She stands in the middle of a raised platform, and cars bang by on either side. Tin can snakes with gray stripes. It is not impossible to jump in front of them. There would be a smash, and then a fall to the hard floor. Most likely a death.

In the dream, Tiny stands in-between the trains for a while. They zoom in opposite directions, and they keep coming, like popcorn from the movie theatre kettle. A black button-up glove lies scrunched on the platform. People hold grocery bags and electric bouquets of yellow roses. Tiny sees babies, dogs with chests round and hard as twenty-five cent toy capsules, and people she could love. They might see her too. She doesn't know for sure. Instead of moving or dying, Tiny just stands there. She stays. It's a dream.

Tiny is probably the hero, because we're spending all this time looking at her.

She would rather not be seen at all. Not be a bug, pinned and spread.

Tiny is so young, but she has already been alive so long. Sometimes it makes her dizzy.

Tiny sees her mother's cancer. It's the color of white corn, sequined with bugs and pulsing heat into the air. Tiny sees it living in the box she didn't watch them shut. She didn't throw dirt or petals on it either. Tiny misses her mother, but doesn't have any memories of her face apart from photographs, which feels like carrying around a hole. Sometimes Tiny stares so long at the pictures they start moving.

Her mom died when Tiny was three. That woman's arms look smooth as moonlight in a cartoon, and soft. Tiny's look the same, so she squeezes them to understand. She hugs herself as two people at once. When she wishes she could have a conversation with her mom, Tiny looks for flowers or eats a bowl of grapes. Any color. She doesn't know why. For a while, Tiny thought her mom communicated through Motown on the radio. Missing someone is hard, always, but the details change. Sometimes it's a spiral. Sometimes a shawl.

Grief is not always sharp, but grief is always.

Grief is playing in the shadow of a familiar house. A house where familiar people ate and slept and loved. Sometimes a person falls asleep in that shadow. Dead-asleep, drool-on-the-grass-asleep, and sometimes in that sleep they dream about the person who left. They wake with leaves smashed into the side of their face, and for three seconds they forget ever missing anyone.

Grief is losing an arm and realizing there is nothing to do about it.

You don't have an arm anymore.

Every morning you think: wow. I don't have an arm.

Naming something doesn't mean you understand it. You need to watch for a while too, and look for patterns. When Tiny started her period, which is one fact about her body, she thought about the rhythm of it. Every month a circle, in the end. An ocean, froth and spit. Sometimes Tiny catches the blood in a cup, to pour on plants outside.

The blood drips down. Descent. Tiny is descending. This means both inheritance and evasion. She pictures herself winding down a staircase, face changing with every step. She pictures joy, depression, and money.

Izzy went to bed, but Tiny is still on the roof. She watches everything outside fringe. Now is an after. Tiny feels water in the corner of her eye, a hinge in her chest. She is exhausted. Tiny crawls back in through the window. Since that window is a door almost every morning too, its paint has started to flake, and the bug screen is torn. Tiny wipes her feet carefully. She takes off her clothes. She lies on top of the sheets in her underwear, like a corpse except her heart is still blooming. A bloom is always itself: a polyvalence, not a parade. It is, and Tiny's brother is dead, again and again.

In the morning Tiny has to decide what to do. It's not really a decision. Rather, she will reckon with her body, which is her mother's and brother's too. Tonight, Tiny sleeps in waves. She stares at the ceiling and imagines a fire starting in her chest. She cries, and it sounds like a silo. The sky outside is blue-pink and starry gold, day and night at once.

Sometimes, Tiny and Izzy talk about how hard it is to not be guys. Guys have it easy. Easier. Sometimes, they dress like guys in slim jeans and flat-front shirts, which is also like wishing puberty never happened. It's like wishing they were still middle schoolers. They slink all over the neighborhood, hips-first and speaking one register lower. They call each other bro. It isn't funny. Tiny and Izzy look at their nails by making small fists instead of stretching out their hands. They talk about music and hunger, and they tell stories that are shaped long and straight. Stories that end clearly and permanently.

These kinds of stories are comforting because, like the weather, they are okay to talk about with pretty much anyone. They are binary operations that many people have seen or solved already. Even if they haven't, their brains know the patterns. They can relate. The pictures are familiar, even watered-down, and any ambient anxiety is calmed by trust in a resolution. Even when it's violent. Even when humans bloom and Tiny's hands, which are alive, are her dead mother's hands too. Even then, these hard, flat stories promise comfort, with plenty left over to tuck away for next time.

Honestly, Tiny just wants to walk down the street without worrying. She and Izzy try it on like a costume. Only ever thinking about yourself is exhausting. A boring coil.

Tiny never read a story about a person like her, but she never wanted one. She never thought to ask. There might be one, somewhere, but Tiny is plenty already. She is more, and so she cannot be anyone else.

The grooves are set.

Here Tiny is, a story in this shimmering body.

In the ancient Greek tragedies we know, death almost always happens offstage. A messenger runs on to tell the audience what happened. Someone rolls out a cart with a body slumped on top. A bloody little diorama. Little means cute, but also nimble and able to survive. Little can tuck into a corner.

The body on the cart might also be limp in a kitchen, or slung on top of sheep. All red, and pulsing at the neck if you look closely enough. Sometimes it's sweaty.

There is solemnity in looking at a body pretending to be dead. Pretending release. It's almost funny, like a kid playing a joke. Because eventually, the lights come back.

With a fake dead body, there are no flies. No muscle spasms, no gut-gas. The audience is not forced to watch the last breath or the moment the eyes dull, or to feel anything about any of it.

This turns death into an object. A reference point. A glow.

It turns death into something anyone could understand or forget.

In ancient Greek theatre, everyone in the audience sits down together, and they look. It's uncomfortable, and it's active. They try to see it together. In real life, fingernails and hair continue to lengthen after death, not because they're growing but because the body is shrinking. It sounds like vines. A last flower.

Tiny and Izzy were neighbors before they were born. Before they were sisters. Their moms drank tea and talked about how right now, our babies are water babies. Their gills will turn into ears and jaws. Tiny was born a little before Izzy, on the first day fall turned a corner and felt cold. Tiny imagines her mom walking down the driveway to the car, yellow leaves scratch-circling like rags about to turn into a gown. A gown, not a dress. Air like cold apples. Tiny doesn't imagine her father there at all, and so he wasn't. It is hard for some people to watch things that their bodies can't do. They feel helpless, and then they are stuck.

Izzy was born a month afterwards, with so much hair her face seemed smaller than it was. After that, their mothers drank more tea. They split cheap bouquets from the grocery store, and they shared casseroles and tips for growing. Tiny and Izzy ate and watched everything together all the time, like goldfish. Eventually, Tiny's mom went back to work at the hospital. Sometimes, Tiny and Izzy slept in the same bed. On the same rug. They lived in one house, split only by grass and cement.

When they were old enough to be alone together, Tiny and Izzy played all day in that in-between space. They were short, which made the grass tall. They played with sidewalk chalk and woolly bear caterpillars, and ornamented the beer dish slug traps with saxifrage. Tiny and Izzy pretended to be color fairies, which means everything you say has to be about color somehow. It's important to play pretend with people you love, because then when disaster happens, you have other memories and options. Once Izzy was blue and all she said was moon moooooon mooon. Months later, she crashed into a signpost on her bike and woke up the next morning with a blue knee. Moooon, said Tiny when she saw, and they laughed.

Tiny and Izzy played pirates and orphans, only the neighbors looked out their windows and didn't understand. They called Izzy's mother and said, your child is tied to the telephone pole with jump rope. She is screaming, and we can't tell if she's really hurt or not. Izzy wasn't. She was trying it out.

Later, Izzy's mother explained to them both that some games need to be private, like when Tiny took off her shirt to read in the sunshine. It wasn't bad, but it was a private thing. Tiny didn't understand. She was the only one playing. No one else felt the breeze on her back, or the grass pressing into her elbows. It was already private.

Sometimes, a world isn't for anyone else. Often, other people's questions about it can't be answered, because they are outside. They are looking at something that might not know they exist, and if it isn't hurting them, for fun or for money, it doesn't need to.

You are the only one who has to answer the worlds built inside your head.

You are the first one who lives in them or leaves.

Sometimes, Tiny and Izzy spent weeks not really talking to anyone but each other. Their first step was always: pretend our mother is dead. By then, Tiny's mother really was, so like that they taught themselves to mourn.

Today, there is a war.

The fighting happens far from where Tiny and Izzy live, so bombs explode inside their heads instead of in the streets. In their streets, everything is the same. Their lights go on at dusk every night like always, and the candy selection at the drugstore is the same. They can still buy dried apricots and pistachios and rugs, if they had the money and wanted to. At the gas station is a big, stay-fresh barrel of Lemonheads that has existed since Tiny and Izzy were tall enough to see over the counter. It's still there. Still available to them.

Inside Tiny's head, her house is bombed almost every night. The office where her dad works is hit first, and then the whole house curls mad red around it. The fact that Tiny's brain does this—her brain hits him first—scares her more than anything. She can see his face. She is horrified that her brain does that, but it isn't a thought she remembers starting. Izzy says it's because Tiny is the helper. Next, she would help him.

There are no sounds in Tiny's dreams, so when she wakes up she adds them, like carding threads back into a sweater. Tiny smells the chemical char. She sees mouths opening so wide necks become mouths too. Izzy thinks about ways to help. She could knit mittens for the soldiers, or put cool handkerchiefs into plastic bags, to use for mopping fluid and sprays. She could make them apple cake, which keeps well in pockets and also has fruit. People can take fruit and cake into a field. When Izzy makes these suggestions, often people think she is too simple, but the reality is that Izzy is a good listener, and so she is good at helping. It is a strength. Izzy helps people in the ways they ask to be helped, which means that she makes them stronger. She cares. Tiny and Izzy talk about the war all the time: what it is, and how they understand it. How afraid they are. Over time, this fear edges into anger. They have never known the world otherwise.

The war is about oil. The far-away country has more than they could use in lifetimes, in generations, and so other countries are fighting to share. To take. Other countries want oil to lube, wax, tar, and cement. To run cars, planes, and buses, and to make plastics. The fighting is awful, which is a factual observation even though Tiny doesn't know anything about specific weapons, or even what the country at war looks like, really. She wouldn't know how to find beans, eggs, or candy in their country. Or flowers or grapes. Tiny wouldn't know where children play color in-between, like she did with Izzy. She doesn't know where people go to work, or what they do. There is a lot to learn. But Tiny has time.

Often, men tell her that asking questions about meals and children means she doesn't understand war at all. Tiny knows they're wrong. They are so wrong, and so late, that they forgot the people. These men wear their bodies like suits, forgetting that bodies are shaped in response to experiences. What's more, pain lives in the body and can be inherited, like hair color—even like red, which is recessive. Tiny imagines the kids in this far-away country, absorbing the assaults and adapting their cells for survival. She thinks the mothers probably understand, but many of them are trapped too.

Tiny remembers when the war started. People were talking on all the televisions with their jaws locked, and tremors in their voices. People on television have money and space to stay calm, and so when Tiny heard the anchors unable to hide their fear she felt scared too, like mud and hair turned suddenly into fulgurite. An electricity. The reality. Tiny wore her hoodie up all day. She chewed its silver zipper until she almost cracked her tooth.

Tiny already knew that a war in any country, but especially in a country that is far away from yours, and poorer than yours, means disaster everywhere. Tiny looks at her friends' faces and imagines them scarred. She frightens herself. There are now weapons that shred skin. There are now weapons that drop viruses into bedrooms.

The war, now, is old.

Tiny's friend Tim went to war. He came back with a metal foot and tuition for two full years of college.

Tiny's friend Alex went to war. He came back with new flavor combinations, an extensive internet roleplaying community, and a government job.

Tiny's friend Stacy went to war. She came back with a husband.

Tiny's friend Frank went to war. He came back with burns on his face, and then he went to war again. When Tiny talked to Frank on the phone, his voice sounded like a stadium, flickering in the hot dark until the main act starts. She wasn't sure how to feel about it.

Soon Tiny started to notice signs in groceries and drugstores. They forced people into two lines, What You Are and What You Are Not, and those lines had different food and medicine available.

In war, there isn't room to be in-between. You are dead, or you are alive, or you are oblivious like a god on a bender. This is the line for veterans, this one for single people, this one for WIC. For one side to have power, the other side must not. This is less hopeless than it sounds, but it is generally true in wars that use bombs, and wars that use unequal wealth, inadequate health care, and other kinds of terror.

Both / and thinking frightens people. So does yes, and.

When someone is already dead, and you look at them again and again, it is an obscenity.

War does this to people.

Tiny's brother went to war.

His name is Kelley.

Say it. Write it in fire. Tell it to the trees. We scream:

K E L L E Y.

Before she sat on the roof, Tiny walked in the woods.
There are strands of wet grass on her jeans.

Before she walked in the woods, Tiny saw the shape in the car.

When Tiny saw the shape in the car, she knew it was bad. She
knew it was Kelley. Only Kelley is an it. Present tense now. He
is a memory, and he is in her body. She can't call him on the
phone. She would be calling herself instead.

Tiny sees the shape in the car and tells herself no. If she turns around, if she shakes her head and walks, she can have the distance of another couple hours. She can still have a brother who ollies on a dime and always comes home with a flower in his belt loop. Bear will find Kelley, find the body instead, and Tiny will never say she already knew.

Then, Tiny, breathing, realizes doing this would erase her body too, and so she walks into the garage anyway. Tiny doesn't turn on the light. Kelley's body is bright enough, it is, the brightness, and besides that Tiny doesn't want to see everything right away. It feels like her brain would shatter and chime and no sense could be made of anything, anymore, ever.

Her second thought is that Meryl, the girl who loves Kelley—Meryl must never see this. Or maybe Meryl should. See this, see it, like the body is not a person. Was never. If the body is not a person, where is Kelley? Tiny doesn't know, but she is sure anyone who is left needs a ritual. Anyone drowning in future memory. Everyone who still has time here, time to wear pants or manage a gentle tinnitus. If people are left, then time exists. If time exists, sometime, a war won't kill everyone. It is possible. Even before the shape in the garage, Tiny knew the war killed Kelley. She couldn't tell how much, but she knew it did. Tiny remembers seventh grade when her class read about a Japanese girl dying from leukemia. The teacher showed them a map about atomic bombs. The destruction shudders out like a spin-dye t-shirt. Suddenly Tiny doesn't care if Meryl sees the body or not. Instead, she wants to make Meryl some food.

Meryl likes peanut butter and marmalade sandwiches, with the crusts cut off like she is a child. We are all children sometimes. In this scenario, Tiny would be the mother. She would cut the bread on a diagonal, differently than usual, so that after Meryl finished the meal and heard the news, she would know that even when everything is different, some things taste the same. She would not know this in words, but maybe that wouldn't matter. Tiny thinks breaking the news over a meal is a good idea, because if your stomach is working, you can't forget your body. The table needs to be cleared, and if you can't do it yet, that is a reminder too. Digestion is the process of taking something that wasn't you, but turning it into you anyway.

Tiny doesn't think she can open the car door, even though her hand is already reaching for it. It's the same old car door, but in the back seat is a shape like her brother. It is like Kelley, but it is not.

Tiny feels big heat coming from inside the car, like leaving the movies in summertime. She is surprised the windows are not foggy. Dead Kelley's neck has an electrical cord wrapped around five times tight, flush underneath the little fist-shape in his throat. Tiny remembers when Kelley didn't have an apple at all. Kelley's eyes went red, and there is a stream of dried blood out his nose. His face looks like an allergic reaction. Tiny can't look at the body through the window anymore. She can't see it.

It's too bright, too radioactive.

When Tiny closes her eyes, she sees the shape.
Sees her brother like sunspots.

Tiny is sure she is more alone now, which makes a horrible buzz.

Tiny thinks: which electrical cord is that, and where do I buy another?

We're missing one now.

She walks outside the garage and barfs into the rhododendron.

Tiny : Once I went to UP IN ARMS alone. I danced, and when someone ordered pizza, we danced the pizza dance, which means you hold a slice in your hand and spin until you can't anymore. You spin so fast the room keeps lurching when you stop. Then you lie on the floor, and you eat. You eat pizza, and you are alone, because no one bothers a girl doing that. It's delicious.

Afterwards, I stood up, and I was ready to go home.

So I walked home in the dark, with my hair blowing into my mouth. I walked home alone in the dark, like everyone does eventually.

Izzy : Sometimes in the dark I close my eyes. It's practice.
I feel a copper band around my heart.

MAIREAD CASE   55

In the same house, Bear is finishing his work at the desk for
the night. Bear is Tiny and Kelley's father. He loved their
mother very much, and he still loves her so much that he can't
let her leave. To him, her presence is a physical requirement
for life as he knows it, like how his shoulder fits in his socket.
How his elbow bends no wider than 180 degrees. Without his
wife, Bear doesn't know exactly who he is, or how to support
his children, growing, and so he keeps everything like when
she was alive. This way, Bear can live like she's just taking a
little longer at the library. Like she went to the grocery store,
or to see Izzy's mom. Tiny's mother's jewelry nests like sea
creatures in velvet boxes on the dresser. Her quiet shoes
sit near the door, their soles clean but darkened with dust,
sweat, and skin. The spices she used still clutter the lazy susan,
sticky-lidded, though now Bear mostly orders out, or eats a
package of cheese and half a can of olives with garlic.

   On his desk, Bear keeps photographs of Kelley and
Tiny as kids, and Izzy too. His wife is not in any of those
photos, but her ghost was, even then. Even when her body
still was. Kelley's knees are reinforced with heavy denim
patches, and Tiny has ribbons tied like speech bubbles in her
hair. His wife sewed them. She braided it. It was her. In every
photo, you could cover everyone's mouth, and from the look
in their eyes alone you could tell how happy they all were.
How safe. How seen, how held. Before he met his wife, Bear

didn't think life could be scheduled, maintained, and enjoyed. He only ever endured it, but with her, he learned it could also be trusted and loved. And so Bear did. He dove in. Sometimes Tiny is overwhelmed with love for her father. It hits her like a smoke curtain and makes her eyes glossy.

Tonight, Bear's son is a shape in the car, and Bear writes a letter to a neighbor whose sixtieth birthday is next week. Bear remembers. Crises don't stop birthdays, anniversaries, or pregnancies. Bear uses heavy cotton paper and a stamp with a caramel-colored heart on it. His handwriting is all one size and shape, with points like blunted stars. It has always been this way. Bear is tender, like his daughter. They are family. They love each other and have never known otherwise.

Bear thinks about his wife. He switches off the big gold lamp in his office, thinks about his wife again, and walks up the stairs to sleep. Bear still sleeps on the right side of the bed. The left is completely made. Tonight, in this house, there are four places for four people to sleep: Bear, Kelley, Tiny, and their mom. His wife. Tonight is the end of that happening in space and time. After this, their family is together elsewhere, later, and always, but never again to eat dinner.

‖ | | |

Tiny almost always believes stories. Everything wants to make sense of the world, or to drift from it. To love in it, as far as someone knew. Since Tiny was little, people have asked who she wants to be when she grows up. But Tiny is already. She is here and ready now. Tiny knows there will be other adventures and times to rest. The order matters.

Listening is crucial. If you hear someone else's story, you have one solution set. If you also have their body, and their exact problem, in time, their solution set might be yours too. It could help you. It might not. When Tiny listens, she is in her head but also the other's, which is hard, so not something many other people actually do. It's an advanced practice. When she's in a room with another, Tiny imagines a third chair, sitting empty. Who might come and sit? Who is missing? The word for lap connects to curve, echo, and sinew, which is how muscles connect to bone. How we bind, held, hold. Stories are arcs, but they are also waves, firecrackers, flowers, and rings. Sometimes they are black holes.

The ancient Greeks believe a person sees because beams of light shoot out their eyes. Tiny agrees that the eye is an optic, but it's also a receptor. Both ways of seeing make sense, but the stories they can tell are different. The Greeks can only ever be the protagonist or the audience, but Tiny can be everyone at once. She is hero, enemy, and peanut gallery. This is a strength, and also it is exhausting.

In her everyday life, Tiny meets lots of people who do things she would like to do. Julie spraypaints beach scenes and tigers on the sides of cars, then disappears for the winter. Theo visits laundromats to collect detergent bottles, and then he dresses like a robot made out of detergent bottles. He visits the summer carnival to pose with people. It is the most lucrative job Theo has ever had. Tiny's friend Emily catches babies in the hospital. She talks about her job like part of it is baseball, part of it is swimming. Part of it's wonder. Tiny's other friend Nora lies inside a cello case during performances. Eventually, people started paying Nora to put them inside the cello cases too. Tiny's friend Curtis fell in love with men and became a priest.

Tiny is here to know them. To know them is to see them and to let them change.

It is exhausting, and also it is overwhelming.

This is why Tiny sits on the roof so much, and why she walks in the mornings. Like this, Tiny keeps herself in her body. She breathes. She protects herself from whiplash.

What does everyone do before they fall asleep? Tiny flosses. She takes hawthorn under her tongue. She claws at her hair. When she was little, Tiny sucked her thumb. She gnawed a little dent in it.

When Tiny's mother was alive, Bear was softer. His body was gentler. There is a picture of them in a pewter frame on the bookshelf. Just married. Bear is wearing a tie over his t-shirt, and his body is lean, not starved of subcutaneous fat like it is now. His smile shows teeth, and until Tiny saw this picture she had forgotten he used to smile another way. Tiny's mother's chin blooms luminous and happy from under a clip-on veil, and her hands are looped around her new husband's waist. He was so excited to marry her he forgot a belt. This, to Tiny, is the mark of true love. She does not want to own anyone, ever. She wants to be so awestruck she forgets significant articles of clothing.

After Tiny's mother died, Bear went to the war. When she was alive, he worked for it instead. This confused Tiny. War as a job. But once Bear's wife died, he needed to be in the same place as the violence. He could not be at home, drinking fresh coffee and reading the paper, now that no place was safe. His wife died. Cities were dying. Now, the war in the far-away country matched the war inside his head. The noise was inside and out. If Bear was the source, he might as well go to it too.

At first Bear told Tiny he went to the war for money, to support her school and the house, and everything. Kelley would take care of her, and so would Izzy and Izzy's mom. Aunt Charlotte would move in for a while, and she did. However, after he came back, Bear admitted he left because he didn't want to be alive without his wife. He finally said it. If Bear died fighting for gasoline, he thought, at least Tiny and Kelley would never be poor. Tiny said that was just as stupid as owning someone. This hurt Bear, and he turned angry, like a tornado touched down on the tallgrass prairie of his brain. Bear said the kitchen lights gave him a headache. Tiny didn't have anything else, so she gave her dad a look and went to sit on the roof awhile. Tiny had meant: Dad, we need you here. He would have responded: I'm trying. I'm trying to protect our family. I do own you, kind of. For now.

Bear still works for the war, but now he's home. Finally he has a job where he doesn't need to wear a uniform, but Bear wears one anyway, from habit, and to communicate his intelligence, impact, and power. Bear, like his love and now his pain, can be trusted. His uniform is an egg-bald head, perfectly circular glasses, and dark ties: midnight, silver, hurt-maroon. Sometimes when he is in the office, Tiny sneaks into his closet and smells them. Bear still wears his wedding ring, because death is not the end. When Tiny is angry with her dad for letting grief and work take over his life, for now, she looks at that ring. It is an ouroboros with one ruby eye, and realistic-looking dents near where its teeth clap into the tail. Tiny imagines her father younger. Her mother in love with him. She imagines not existing at all. Tiny's mom said people can't make you angry unless you let them.

We see Bear in this story, but we do not see him intimately because there are already lots of books about Bears.

This is a book about Tiny.

Talk with people who have different kinds of money and power

Talk with people without trying to make them all the same

                              or feeling sorry for them

                              Pity can be violent, do the work

          Question gatekeepers

              & validity

      Ask for yourself

      Expect parentheses   &

                                        &

                      &   &

  &   &

              &   &

  &

                                      &

&

Let it vanish

The good places must flux

Count the steps, the trails from where you are to your friends

Humans estimate that snails spend up to twenty-five percent of their energy making mucous trails for travel. However, if they're following a path another snail already made, it takes less energy.

Tiny takes a different path through the woods every day.

Tiny and Izzy like to go dancing, but not everywhere. They dance at one group night. It started in the back of a shop that also sells pho. First they ate in the front, at a table covered in off-white cloth, topped with glass and bottles of soy. In the beginning, Tiny and Izzy put everything into their pho. White worm bean sprout tangles, holy basil, fish sauce, and noisy limes. They squirted hot red paste into the broth. It looked pretty next to their gold nail polish and orchestral bracelets. Like eating was also a plot. Like to understand everything, you have to taste it.

Later, Tiny and Izzy learned what they liked. After eating, they crunched a peppermint, walked away from the families eating dinner, through the swinging pink-red-purple bead curtains, and they danced.

Tiny dances slunk-low to the ground, like she is hiking and afraid of losing her balance. She does not make eye contact with anyone except Izzy.

Izzy looks at everyone. She uses her hands like they are also sock puppets saying yeah all of the time. Yeah. Yeah!

The night is produced by three people who are a couple years older than Tiny and Izzy. Thuy, Marnie, and Shawn all have jobs that start in the evenings. Those jobs aren't a part of the dance night, which is also a job. Thuy grew up in the pho restaurant. Their eyes match the women in the front room, but their body is flatter and electrified, like they stuck a finger in a socket a long time ago and healed. They wear suit jackets. Sometimes they paint shapes onto their face. Izzy is in love with Thuy, but secretly. It is a gentle agony.

Sometimes Tiny and Izzy walk home, or Hank picks them up, but sometimes Tiny rides the bus alone. When she does, Tiny looks at the sun for an extra-long time. She watches its color heat the sky like a chicken in an oven. When Tiny dances at night, she never feels lonely. She doesn't miss her mother, and she doesn't think about time at all.

when Tiny was sixteen her brother kil

himself

Death is always a disaster. It u

In the desert, animals sleep through the hottest days. Sheep can live without water for at least thirty-six hours. Afterwards, they find a source, guzzle it, and are fine. Rats take water from seeds and pass dry pellets. They pass shells. Seeds in, pellets out.

What if Tiny grew a body apart from her grief? To help her hold on through it? The rest of her would be different, but okay.

Once the situation is stable, people can talk about what's next. They can plan. Sometimes it's easier, quicker, or temporarily necessary to pretend that everything's stable. But when it isn't, when that is being faced, you have to separate yourself from yourself to imagine a future. That can make you sick, or it can make you a flower.

folds

The morning after she found the body, Tiny took another walk. Afterwards, Tiny slips out of her shoes and into the kitchen. Aunt Charlotte is not really Tiny's aunt, but she is here. Charlotte is an old friend of Tiny's mother. They grew up together like Tiny and Izzy are now. The sunburns Charlotte and Tiny's mother had now echo across Tiny and Izzy's bodies. It's the same sun. When Tiny's mother died and the war came to Bear, Aunt Charlotte moved into the studio out back. It isn't clear whether anyone asked her to or not. Aunt Charlotte and Bear only talk to each other about practical things, like house project lists and if Tiny will make herself sick with all that sad music. No, Charlotte always says. She won't. Tiny is moving through her feelings.

Aunt Charlotte's small house is next to an abandoned laundry line, a swing and glide, and a patch of onions that Tiny and Izzy used to pick when they played casting spells. Good spells only. Don't make your body a vector for hate. Tiny and Izzy liked how the onions smelled like bitter pepper. Like bitter flowers. There is no plumbing in this house, just a bed and a studio. It is painted purple, a color Tiny feels in the top of her head.

In her house, Aunt Charlotte paints huge watercolors of the sea and the sky. First, she adds water to acrylic until it looks like washing detergent with bleach. Then, she stripes every color, side-by-side in one layer each. The finished paintings don't look thick. The paint actually mixes with the canvas, like rain falling onto the ground and then it is all one thing. Tiny's favorite is huge and red. Aunt Charlotte says she'll have it as her wedding present, so Tiny knows she will never have it. She does not want to get married. This is a fact, not a feeling. At night when Tiny can't sleep, she imagines houses she'll never live in, and then the rooms in these houses where the painting would hang. It isn't an angry exercise. It calms her.

Aunt Charlotte is making breakfast for herself. When Kelley and Tiny were little, sometimes she would make breakfast for all four of them: Tiny and Kelley, and Tiny's mom and Aunt Charlotte, and sometimes Izzy too. Bear sat with them, but he ate his own food. On special mornings, Aunt Charlotte made bacon in paper towels, toast with butter and cinnamon, and eggs cooked in the microwave, because their smell makes her gag. Now Tiny eats this meal for dinner when she is lonely. It is special forever.

When Tiny's mother died and Aunt Charlotte moved in for real, she never pretended to be the mom. Instead, she cared, enduringly. She checked Tiny's bangs for smashed parts, taped songs off the radio, and made sure no one ever ran out of toilet paper. Now, for breakfast, Aunt Charlotte drinks one cup of coffee with milk, and one green drink. Sometimes the two glasses make Tiny sad. Sometimes Tiny wonders if Aunt Charlotte lives in their house because she's too weak to live on her own, but then Tiny remembers people live everywhere, for all kinds of reasons. Sometimes Tiny's brain is rude to people, instead of accepting that they care about her.

There are cherries, says Aunt Charlotte, right
when Tiny sees them in the bowl, and cereal and milk. The
cherries are perfect, honey. Aunt Charlotte doesn't ask Tiny
where she was, because she is here now. Tiny pours shredded
wheat in a coffee mug and sits at the creaky old table with the
yellow-glitter top. The green drink has a straw, and when Tiny
watches Aunt Charlotte drink it she wants to hug her. Aunt
Charlotte always wears the same color of lipstick. Between red
and pink, but different than her paintings. Tiny isn't hungry.
She looks at her hands on the table. She holds a cherry and
expects it to pulse. An artery from the sun.

Antigone is a play written by Sophokles around 441 B.C.E. Reading it is like building a bouquet. Many people translated the story, so readers can gather and gather, and eventually their arms are full of flowers. The arrangement is different, in different times and seasons, and so it is important, though not absolutely necessary, to remember that once they are in your arms, these flowers are missing soil and water. They are bodies. They need context for weight. However, a bouquet in an empty room is still a bouquet. So are the petals blown-out before winter, or left on the floor of a church.

In the original version, Antigone is Ismene's sister. They have a nurse, who is probably a slave, and two brothers, Eteokles and Polyneikes, who fought and killed each other in a civil war. Now the brothers are two bodies, dead in the dust. *Thuddddddhh.* Their mouths are dry. They are lying in blood, which mixes into sand and turns it all into mud. Which bakes in the sun. It smells. Now their uncle, Kreon, is the king.

Kreon refuses to let anyone bury Polyneikes. (Who else was left outside the city walls to bake into the dust? To lose eyeballs to birds? Slaves.) But Antigone buries Polyneikes anyway. She buries him because she loves him, and because she doesn't want him to die a slave.

The entire story happens in one day, and when it starts Polyneikes is already dead.

A plot would be a distraction. A palliative measure.

In ancient Greece, slaves were everywhere. They were born into slavery, exposed into it, or captured. They were supervised by women, and dead-named by their masters. There were more slaves than free people. Police were slaves. So were banking clerks and the navy.

This is the only part of the book that uses the word slave. Does that mean the slaves are gone?

You, arms full of flowers, could tell this story without mentioning Haimon. Haimon is Hank, is Kreon's son and Antigone's love. It is interesting how, as the translations soften, so could Hank. Of course, he doesn't. Why would they erase the boy. The one who turns Antigone from a child into a wife. It isn't death that does it.

After Antigone buries her brother, Kreon buries her. Alive. At the last minute, Haimon crawls in there with Antigone. There are cracks in the translations, like there are cracks in the tomb. Peek inside and see Antigone and Haimon lying together. Their feet are bare. They are telling each other a story about the future.

Sometimes you can pretend your way out of mourning. Sometimes Tiny sleeps with earplugs, like when she shared a wall with Kelley. He played records late at night. Songs about modern guys and falling in love. Tiny can't fall asleep around drums, so she stuffed her ears instead of asking Kelley to turn it off. The earplugs feel like when Tiny used to suck her thumb. Her ears are her mouth.

Sometimes mourning is the longest bus ride. You're fine. You're fine, but then you stand up and you desperately need a bathroom. It is half-nausea, half-ache. An impending release. It is all of these things at once.

Tiny wishes there was an official uniform for mourning. Not so people would ask more questions, but so they could understand. Then, at first people could offer water and patience instead of space and looks. Tiny imagines it like a forest fire index. Death scientists could measure dryness based on rainfall and evaporation, with wind speed, temperature, and humidity as variables. Then death scientists could deduce how sad you are and offer sounds and textures for it. They would look at the data and help. Forests can grow back after burns. The soil stays rich.

It is spring now too, so the forests are full of spring oats and cereal rye. Moss is everywhere, like always, one cell thick but loudly alive on fallen logs and open face rock. Tiny walks through the green ideas. Imagining hands pulling her down into water. Imagining her body letting them think they have her. They don't.

Tiny doesn't know who they are, but she's always imagined walking through them anyway. Tiny keeps her thumb outside her fist. The most important thing, Hank taught her, is not to stop when you hit the other person's face. Don't freeze. What if they don't have a face? Tiny asked, and Hank looked at her with a soft smile. You keep going, he said. This is one reason why Tiny loves Hank. He helps her prepare for everything, even the things that don't yet exist outside her head.

Tiny doesn't like sitting still unless she's on a roof or up a tree, so she doesn't wait in any one place for Hank to pick her up in his classic paste-brown car. Tiny never wears headphones in the forest, but on the way to school, which is lined in concrete and traffic lights, she slips in one earbud. Down we go, cradle and all, Tiny sings aloud. She swings her arms. Down we go. Tiny likes music that makes her body feel like lava. Like she has to shake iron parts from her fingertips. Once Tiny read an article about a man who had magnetic finger implants. When he was near microwaves, his fingers started to hum. He said it made touch feel like hearing. When Tiny dances, she thinks about this man. She shakes her fingers to attract all the crushed soda cans and rusted washers in the world. No one is united, Tiny hums. All things are untied. Tiny doesn't actually think that's true, but it feels that way sometimes. She loves the song anyway. It helps her get a feeling out.

There is only one road between Tiny's house and the school, so Hank finds Tiny easily, every time. Today he picks her up after the convenience store with its giant glossy vape posters, before the place that sells wacky operating room scrubs. Once Tiny went inside when she was stoned and looked at the pawprint ones for twenty minutes. On the road, Tiny is usually lost in thought, so Hank slows the car and cracks his window. Hi, he says. Tiny is always glad to see Hank, even when her brain is full of other things. His hair is number seven fresh and she runs her fingers through it, gently. It is a high maintenance haircut, and he maintains it.

The classic paste-brown car belongs to both Hank and his dad. Hank drives it most of the time, to school and to his basketball coaching job at Luna Elementary, but when his dad has a DJ night he drives it instead. Hank's dad doesn't drink anymore, so when he is ready to get home after a gig, he really is ready. The bus wouldn't work. Drinking is one way to deal with anxiety and public energy, and another way is costuming. Right now Hank's dad is into costuming. Their back seat is draped in blue feather boas with waterproof daisies, strap-on pearlescent wings, tubes of rainbow paint, and faux fox tails. Hank is a little embarrassed by it, but he's proud of his dad. His dad figured out what he needed to do to stay.

Hank insists on listening to classical piano in the car, because it is generally separate from DJ nights, and that makes the space his own. When Tiny listens to Hank's piano music, she imagines a man walking up a staircase, and up it and up it and up it again. She is glad to see her boyfriend, and kisses him in the soft salt-spot behind his right ear. Tiny gets a little hair in her mouth. She presses her tongue to her wrist so she can see it too.

Keep me safe, Tiny says sometimes.

Inside her head or on paper.

Keep me safe, and set me free.

Hank made Tiny a necklace. It started with a meteorite. It fell, and then Hank put in an order and someone else wrapped it with tissue paper and tape. Tiny is amazed Hank paid for stars. It is not something she would do. She would not pay for anything from the sky, but Hank did, and that makes him a cowboy. He lassoed it for her and brought it home. Hank heated the star to stick to four little loops of silver, which he knows Tiny likes because four makes a field. A mass, instead of an either / or. Instead of choosing between two things, you can lie down in the dirt awhile. You can look up at the sky and think about your choices, and whether or not they fit you. For now, or in the future. For the next person.

When Hank gave her the necklace, Tiny imagined tossing up the star. Letting it go again. She believes dead cold things still have heat, have movement, even though she could never draw the map. She could draw a guess, but it would not be exact. Tiny hung the star in the baldhip rose in the forest. She hasn't shown her altar to Hank yet. If she does, Tiny knows it will be right before she leaves for good.

Hank made Tiny that necklace. This is something she loves about him. Hank isn't afraid of fire. He thinks fire is a way to change. Hank smokes chocolate-colored cigarettes long as middle fingers. Tiny imagines the cloves and glass floating into her own lungs too. It's a dark comfort. Tiny is brave, but also she is afraid of dying at different times than the people she loves. How will she ever find them again. Her own death is besides the point. She is not afraid of that. She wishes she was less afraid of loneliness. It's different than being alone.

Here is another thing Tiny loves about Hank: if the world did come to an end, if their bodies survived the flames and dust and insects scuttling, Hank would know how to make a roof. He could tell Tiny when it was okay to swim, and meanwhile he would build things from old wood and tin. Machines Tiny couldn't imagine until she used them, or they carried her. This is how Hank knows to be in love. He imagines the worst thing, then making a life together anyway. Tiny knows Hank will never leave her, and she will never leave him unless something else is bigger. She knows the something will not be a person, which makes being with Hank like preparing for war.

When a bone fractures, at first the bone bleeds. The blood clots and meshes in the break.

Then e v e r y t h i n g swells, bringing stem cells, bone marrow, and more blood to the healing stress point.

Soon cartilage begins to form, at the edges of the fracture first.

Eventually soft callus is replaced by hard callus, and finally, three to four weeks after the break, there is new bone.

In a mourning-haze, Tiny researches inky black flowers. She doesn't want any. Where would they grow? Also, Kelley would have hated them. He liked yellow flowers and white ones.

Tiny just wants to know what black would look like.

What is a black garden.

Queen of the Night tulips are translucent cups of blood. Black roses look blacker in cool weather. Hellebore needs patience.

Tiny thinks about moss. How it grows in the break. In time, it traps seeds, and then they grow in it too. It becomes their home. Tiny knows because she's seen it.

Tiny would like to wear a hat, big as a cake and dripping with petals, so that the white-noise ache in her shoulders would have a reason that wasn't Kelley.

She can take off a hat.

Kelley died in the front seat.

The car is still wood-paneled. Still dark blue.

There are still quarters and pinecones in the cup holder, and a carbonated juice bottle on the floor. Kelley probably meant to recycle it. Tiny could not tell you any of these details herself.

When she remembers everything, it's one inky hum. A before and after. A horror.

The people who run the dance night with Thuy are Marnie and Shawn. Marnie has red hair from a box, which is important because she likes to talk about it. How to make it last. Marnie likes beauty people can point to. She wears deep-v shirts and taps glitter onto her shoulders. Izzy likes hugging Marnie, because then the glitter is in her hair too, and in the morning it is also a memory. Marnie uses glitter that dissolves in the ocean. It doesn't make the fish sick. Every few weeks, she comes to work wearing all denim, no makeup, and zero jewelry, except for one long silver chain with a big green stone. It's a real stone. When Tiny asks where it's from, Marnie says she doesn't like to say. On those nights the music feels less like spikes, more like circles bobbing together, atomic and gossamer.

Most of the time, Shawn stays behind the counter with the music. Thuy and Marnie help him carry the milk crates, headphones, and mixer inside, and once everything is set, Shawn just listens. He stands behind the decks like a frozen warlock god. Shawn told Tiny he feels the music inside his body, like he is a cup for it. He closes his eyes and feels stars, colors, and ocean water. Sometimes Tiny brings Shawn a paper cone from the sports drink dispenser. The music is too loud to say anything, but Shawn always drinks it all and puts his hand on his chest as a thank you.

One night, Shawn's mom and his auntie, who are twins, came to dance. They held their shoes in their hands and were the last people on the floor. Shawn's auntie had an old photo of him in her purse. It was printed in the upper left corner of an entire sheet of computer paper. She showed it to everyone, and everyone said Shawn looked exactly the same. Tiny likes this fact. Shawn's toddler self and his DJ self are the same, and his auntie knows it.

The dance night is UP IN ARMS, and it has three rules. There are other rules that aren't written, like: be nice. No hate. Hate is not even allowed to exist as sound or thought. The vision of hate turns immediately to vapor.

People who think rules like that are unnecessary have never been surprised by nazi signs inked on a stranger's leg. Usually they come along later, once the rules are so old they seem ordinary. It's like learning to wash clothes. Eventually a person just does it.

The first ARMS rule is: consent is powerful. It matters.

The second is: all gender expressions are welcome. This is an action.

> Tiny remembers a song she used to loop. The chorus was: Are you a girl or a boy? Are you a boy or a girl? The singer's voice was soft, and they sung boy with one or two syllables, depending on the space and the day. Bo-oy. On the recording, it was two syllables. Gender is not always a yes or no question, and so sometimes that song sounded like a health ritual. Sometimes it was an accusation or a question.

The third is: everyone uses whatever bathroom they want. This is obvious. It's easy.

As a result,
in the beginning,

Tiny and Izzy carried brass knuckles in their pockets, because ARMS sounded violent, and they were young. But soon they realized they felt safer at ARMS than anywhere else. Tiny and Izzy realized that never, at any point, could they have pointed at anyone or anything that ever felt threatening at ARMS. They might have been weirded out, but that's different.

Once, Kelley picked Tiny and Izzy up at one-thirty in the morning. He saw their rings glint in the rear view and raised his eyebrows. Kelley asked when they learned to use knucks. Tiny said we don't. We keep them in our pockets. Well, that's a problem, Kelley said. That's a lot to carry around. If something did go wrong, Kelley asked, would you know who to talk to about it? We would, said Tiny. We're never alone there, said Izzy.

Now Izzy's knuckles are in her ribbon box.
Tiny's are at the bottom of the river.

When she was younger, Tiny borrowed Kelley's razor and made two small cuts on the inside of her left ankle. It wasn't abusive or for attention. Tiny wanted to know how cutting felt, instead of only ever imagining it. She knew it wasn't going to be a pattern. She used her non-dominant hand. The blood welled up like orcas cresting in slow-motion, and Tiny was so mesmerized by them that she forgot to close the bathroom door.

Kelley walked by, one with his headphones. He saw Tiny with the razor, and without saying anything, Kelley scooped her into a yellow towel big as the sun. It was warm from the dryer, and Kelley smelled like diesel. He put antibiotic cream on the cuts and said he knew it was hard. Kelley thought Tiny was cutting herself because she missed their mom. Tiny was pretty sure he was wrong, but she didn't try to explain herself. Instead of thinking, Tiny sat safe inside the towel, watching her brother's hands.

Death happens every day. Tiny's mother dies every day.
So does Kelley.

Every day Tiny wakes up and thinks, my mother is dead.
Kelley is dead.

My body is here.

Sometimes she sleeps with one hand on her breast.

Eventually Tiny grows sea legs. She thinks about the mermaid
who lost her family and her voice for love. How, to be free, you
have to give up a part of yourself, over and over again. You
have to be open to change. Might the mermaid have preferred
everyone just came to her in the ocean instead, as they were?
Sure. But the center cannot hold. A lot of people think that
means: get used to disappointment, but it doesn't. It means:
we have bodies. We're in an ecosystem in time. We're alive,
real, and material.

The table is never just a table. To insist that it is means ignoring who made it, and what happens at it.

Its uses. The view from all sides. The animal, hiding underneath.

Mourning can be an incessant humming in the ears. In the chest.
You get used to it, but you never forget it's there.

Tiny thinks more about the mermaid who gave up her tail, her sisters, and all the lights she ever knew for love. She agreed to that. Tiny probably wouldn't make that wager, but she'll never have to. Its world doesn't exist for her.

One Saturday at UP IN ARMS a woman with astral gray hair came to dance with her boyfriend, who looked slick and distant. The woman wore an ankle-length dress like a waterfall and soft orange lips. It was winter. The woman told Marnie she took pills to have a good time. She hadn't had one in so long. This was her night. Her boyfriend was supposed to be guarding her, but Tiny could tell he wasn't doing a good job. Soon he started following Izzy around, but not in a creepy way. An abandoned one. He was probably overwhelmed, and maybe Izzy looked like someone. Meanwhile, the woman started dancing next to Tiny. It was okay. Tiny liked watching her shoulders sparkle. They were dancing together loosely, like one person has one mirror-point in their body and the other has another. Connected, but not a pair. Their eyes kept catching. You are lovely, the woman kept saying. This is so lovely. Tiny said yes. Yes.

After that they didn't talk, but they stayed close. Shawn played a song like a velvet cape with pearls sewn into it. Tiny thought about how to fishhook a clavicle. It wasn't violent, more like pieces locking into wholes. Like a good fit. When Tiny looked at the woman's face again, her eyes were spinning. Spinning isn't bad, but a sudden change to it can be. Tiny asked the woman if she wanted air, and the woman said yes, but cloudily, like she couldn't recognize Tiny after dancing half an hour together.

Outside, they each sat on a side of the rubber slush mat, and Tiny rubbed the woman's back. Tiny was annoyed the slick boyfriend wasn't out there with them, but ultimately that wasn't her problem. She couldn't solve it if she tried. The woman said her name, which Tiny couldn't hear, and Tiny said, hi. I'm Tiny. Then the woman barfed all over the sidewalk. The barf was leafy purple and orange, like a cat ate flowers and couldn't digest them.

I feel better now, the woman said, wiping her mouth on the back of her hand. She stood up and went inside. Tiny sat, thinking and watching the vomit freeze. Suddenly, she thought about cops, and the neighbors, and so she went inside to ask for help. They handed her a kettle and rags and asked if she knew where the hose was, and the hot plate. Tiny said yes. She did. While Tiny was waiting for the water to heat, a person came up. They had a scar on their eyebrow. Tiny wanted to kiss them immediately, the person and their eyebrow, and then Tiny wanted to melt from self-consciousness. She realized she hadn't said anything aloud yet.

Hello, said the person. Do you need help?

Hi, Tiny said. I'm Tiny. I don't, but you can stay if you want.

Hank said okay. I'm Hank. He asked Tiny if she wanted any fruit leather, and it was grape so she said yes. They split it. They learned they liked some of the same things, like the smell of saltwater and puppets with eyelids, and they lived close to each other. Hank carried the kettle outside, and they poured it over the barf, and the barf liquified enough to push down the sewer with a broom. Thanks, said Tiny. Hank said it wasn't a problem. They never saw the woman again, or her boyfriend, but now they were Hank and Tiny. Tiny and Hank.

Tiny does not care why Kelley did it. That Kelley is gone. She knows why and she doesn't, for always now. The situation, meaning exactly what part of him died in the war and what part came home, alive, used to be a knot. She thought she could untie it in time. Now it is a mist.

Tiny read there's always a message people who suicide mean to communicate. Meant. A message they need heard, so they don't dehydrate like a slug in salt. The awful part is sometimes others did hear, but they couldn't do anything. They tried, but they couldn't fix it. They didn't see how. Sometimes, after the person dies, the people left are paralyzed or obsessed. Sometimes they become a child again, or just quiet.

Tiny knew Kelley's message was simply that he was horrified, so horrified. She tried to explain that minutes are states of mind. States of mind can change. Still, Tiny saw Kelley was slipping away to another planet. Another plane. Kelley tried to believe his sister, but that exhausted him too. No plot. Just exhaustion.

Kelley's message was also that the war was wrong. Is wrong. He said it all the time, people heard him, and yet the war still was. Kelley made other suggestions to solve problems the war started and maintained. Please, he said. Now. Let's do this together. Eventually Kelley's life was wholly defined by this struggle, which he could not see ending, and that was a life Kelley didn't want. He didn't want it like how an engine doesn't want bleach. He just couldn't.

Tiny would never argue with her brother about his choices. People will say she is in shock, and she is, but even before that she knew not to argue with him. Tiny will never say she was surprised that Kelley wanted to die. It was clear.

The door is open.

A body in the car.

The radio is on but the volume is all the way down, like Kelley changed his mind, or the song was too much. When Tiny thinks about the radio, she remembers death is only a before and after to the people after. There is a card duct-taped to Kelley's chest. Without looking, Tiny knows it's Saint Dymphna and her wobble-awkward sword. That patient basket of lilies. Tiny thinks Dymphna is boring. She cared so much about virginity, and like: why let someone else decide you're not a kid?

Kelley always said no, Tiny. She heals people. Dymphna relieves them. Kelley and his faith, which he gripped when their mom died. He probably thought he'd see her next. His mom. Where are they. Unlike Tiny, Kelley could remember their mother's voice. In this minute, Tiny knows she will always miss her brother, miss him like the moon is moon is moon. But she will not be angry about that, unless it's how she stays alive sometimes. This is a promise Tiny makes for herself. To herself, and no one else. Tiny will stay alive to see them again. Whatever that looks like. Right now, she can't know. Tiny will stop the warp and weft of this grief.

This is her wager.

Tiny didn't think she could open the car door, but now here she is. She expects a violent smell, a smell that will coat her hair forever, but instead there is a wall of the citrus oil Kelley sprays after Meryl smokes, plus something else that lands like a rock.

Tiny is dizzy and sits down on the floor outside the car. Then she can't smell anything, at all, and so Tiny wonders if her smell died too.

On the roof again, Tiny felt unbelievably sad. She couldn't believe how sad she felt. It snuck up like a fire door closing suddenly to protect a lab. Tiny could not believe how sad she was, and yet she had to believe it.

Tiny didn't cry. Her eyes felt like clogged mustard containers. She laid back on the roof and tried to catch her breath. The sky was a heavy gray, the kind that lets you know morning is closer than before. Izzy was probably across the way.

Tiny can't think of anything she's afraid of now. Nothing. There is none.

Tiny is beautiful. She knows it, not because of magazines or her parents, or even because of Izzy, but because Tiny trusts herself. Of course, this could not have happened without her family, but it is also a hardness, an increased mineral mass from not expecting any certain ending to her life. It's from seeing people and asking them questions about themselves, then trusting these answers. It's from letting Tiny's self change too.

Because Tiny is already here. She is already good.

Tiny's hair is too short to tangle. After showering, she combs it with her fingers, and it's dry by the time she zips her jeans. Tiny's hair makes people notice her eyes. When they stand behind her, many people think Tiny isn't a girl. She doesn't correct them. Some days they're right. Tiny's body is really a boat. She feels like a boat. When Tiny stands, she is all lines and angles. A geometry of elbows. Turn sideways and disappear. Anchor, float on.

Tiny understands herself as a person with many arms, not someone who grows to hold. Who buds. Buds like potatoes, unearthed but growing new limbs in the dark. They sprout, and the sprouts mold. Tiny does not like babies, but she likes making faces at them. Making them laugh. They stick out their tongues. Sometimes Tiny dreams one morning she will stand up and walk off towards the sea. A wanderer headed marine west. If she was, Tiny really could jump. She could jump off a cliff, and her body would water away.

When Tiny was a baby, her dad was nearly always physically present. He cared about Kelley and Tiny so much, and Izzy, and so he tended to them like plants. When Tiny was a baby, on Saturday mornings after his shower, Bear would keep her on his chest. She remembers sitting on him, one big safe island with a tiny bump on it. Bear smelled like pencil shavings and mouthwash. He wore a medallion around his neck, and he would put it in his mouth and look at Tiny and spit it out. She sputtered and clapped, and Bear did it again and again. Tiny loved this game. She remembers it as movement before the existence of time.

Bear's money lets him stop the world. His socks never have heel holes. His underwear is always clean and white, and he can access fresh fruit. If either one turns gray, he buys more. Bear owns a home, so he can stay and do whatever he wants to there. He could fill it with meatballs. He could cover it in felt. Bear can build fences and use water and pesticides. He eats dinner at a certain time every night, because he can, and because he cares. These things in combination mean people pay attention to Bear. It also means people take his advice. Other wealthy men are afraid of sex and death, so they use their money to squirt chemicals into their foreheads. To peel warts off their hands. They use their money to keep themselves from dying. Bear just tells Tiny he loves her. It is an action, and a fact. He means it both ways.

In a corner of Bear's office, next to the photos of Kelley and Tiny, and their mother, and Izzy, there is the bear Tiny used to hold at night. You press a button in his chest, and he tells you a story. Tiny told herself her own stories, but she sucked the bear's nose too. He doesn't have a face anymore, but he could still tell stories perfectly. If anyone wanted that. The technology is good as new.

Tiny remembers the night she and her dad went to Thuy's mom's place for pho. Bear didn't know it was also a place for dancing, but that detail wasn't important to their good time together. Tiny was so happy she wanted to take a picture, even though the restaurant was dark. The picture would have been gold, and green, and pink shadows.

This food is delicious, said Bear, and Tiny smiled. She told him a story about photography class. The assignment was to take a picture of eggs, or an egg, alone on a white background. Tiny used a telephone cord, and Hank used plain spaghetti. Tiny and her dad finished with cream puffs. It wasn't a dance night, so after dinner Tiny hugged Thuy and went home with Bear to sleep.

When they got home, Kelley's door was closed, but his light was on and Tiny heard his music. Here we all are, she thought: anxiously, tenderly. We're all still here. They were, and they were in love.

For now, Tiny knows her body is meant to be. It exists in time and space. She's known this since she was little and climbed trees barefoot, scooting up trunks with her insteps and pressing her face into leaves. In the fall, Tiny wears wool socks and stuffs her feet into clogs. In winter, her calluses shed, and in spring, they grow back. At the tops of the trees, some part of Tiny's brain wants to jump, but her body always says no. Nope. Not yet. You need to last. She doesn't know why she needs to last. She does know that imagining something is one way of actually doing it.

Sometimes Tiny has nightmares of her body, on its face on the grass. If you jump, you'll crumple. Doll-flat. Loose in the green. Tiny isn't sure if the nightmares are a warning or a vision, so to stay calm she sits on the floral sofa, hands on her knees. She breathes. She watches the light stretch across the carpet and stays inside her warm-blooded body like it is a blanket. A shelter. Like her heart is a small fire. It is already a fist. Her heart is brown, and yellow, and red and pink.

This knowing, this refusal to ghost, is a gift from Tiny's mother. The cancer ate her brain, and now Tiny wants to stay alive as long as possible so she can tell her mom, and now Kelley too, what they missed. Tiny believes in spirits but also bodies. Spirits don't have bodies. This is what defines a spirit. People scare Tiny more than ghosts. Sometimes Tiny's heart is an accordion stretched wide. She knows her mom will explain that feeling to her someday.

Tiny talks to her mother at night, sees her swirled, but during the day Tiny is alone. Her mother isn't around any corners, and the objects she left don't smell any certain way anymore. When Tiny's mother died, Bear paid people to clean the house very well, so there aren't even any strands of hair or fingernail clippings left behind. Tiny used to imagine finding a hangnail and turning it back into her mother. When she came back in off the roof after seeing the car, Tiny ate a snarl of hair from Kelley's brush.

If Tiny never slept and never died, she'd never see her mother again. This doesn't make it any easier to sleep. It hurts, missing someone with your body not your mind. Tiny doesn't like nighttime. Right now, she believes in loss more than mystery. When the sun rises it's a relief.

Tiny has a brother too. She still has him. Her mother gave birth to him. His name is Kelley, and he already resisted being a monster. He used cigarettes and sex, and needles lit with a match then dipped in ink. Her family didn't understand why Kelley marked his body and poured smoke into it. They thought he was mutilating himself, but Tiny always knew he was settling in. Bodies are hard. Sometimes wearing one feels like dying instead. Kelley's arm says NO GODS in stutter text, and there is an X on his wrist. Tiny does not know what it means, but she imagines treasure is buried underneath. Like slicing open Kelley's arm reveals rubies instead of blood. When she was little, he'd say do you want to play hide and go seek? He would hide her in the dryer, then come back in ten minutes and say, I found you! Later Tiny realized this wasn't how everyone played, but she was never angry about it. She felt special whenever Kelley found her again.

Kelley has three plaid shirts. One is mustard, one heavy forest, one headache orange. The collars are stained where they touch the back of his neck, because of the hair gel Kelley wears. It smells like coconut and red stripes. Kelley likes eating those plastic cracker packets with fixed cheese and a stick for spreading it. He wears a waxed cord necklace with a poured metal infinity clasp. It rests inside his sternum notch like a kid in a cradle. Tiny used to smear a drop of Kelley's deodorant under her nose so she could smell him all day. It felt safer. To Tiny, Kelley's body has always been safe. Thinking about it still is. Now hers is the closest she has.

One Saturday a boy gave Tiny and Izzy pink pills and they both freaked out, so Tiny went to the twenty-four hour drugstore and bought a stick of Kelley's deodorant. When she smelled it, Tiny knew she could take care of Izzy. She could walk them both home to sleep. And she did. They came home. This is how powerful Kelley is.

Meryl always loved Kelley. She never said it, but Tiny knows the look in her eyes. As long as Tiny has known Meryl, she has had that look. When Meryl looks at Kelley, you could ask her what color is the sky and she'd say wait, what? They sleep together sometimes. Meryl works at the movie theatre, and sometimes when she picks up Kelley after work, she brings Tiny a bag of old popcorn. The bag is splash-decorated and crushed in a tight roll at the top. The butter they use dries in clumps like cat litter. Tiny likes eating those pieces last. She lets the salt shock her throat. Sometimes Meryl acts like she is Tiny's older sister, because it's an excuse to see Kelley. Meryl could just ask to see him, but Tiny doesn't mind the drama. Everyone feels sorry for Kelley and Tiny because their mom died, and so people invent presents and activities. The difference is that Meryl would love Kelley even if his mom was alive. Even if his mom was famous, or a dump truck driver or an angel.

Meryl has slinky-curl brown hair, hands like paper airplanes flying slow along breeze, and acne scars on her cheeks. Once Meryl let Tiny paint the scars into flowers. Each crater was its own disc, and the petals were turquoise eye pencil. Her right cheek turned into a field of cosmos. Meryl likes indigo scarves. Sometimes she makes her own from cloth dunked in big matte vats in the sunshine. Kelley does not love Meryl back, but he likes her a lot. He does not love anyone yet, and maybe he never will. Meryl thinks this is because Kelley and Tiny don't have a mother. No one argues with her because cancer is hard enough already.

Kelley can't talk about cancer at all. He can barely talk about the war, which is why he still lives with Tiny. Why he takes long walks at night. Because Kelley and Tiny live with him, Bear hears doors opening. Thunks and wildflowers dropping, all night long and into the morning. It's a dance. Death is a metal band nobody knows how to hear yet.

But also, Kelley is dead.

He's dead.
He died.

Kelley died.

Tiny loves Meryl because Meryl loves
Kelley.

Also, Meryl has whole lives that have
nothing to do with Kelley, or being in
love with anyone at all.

Meryl worked at an ice cream place that
made its own waffle cones. Her job was
making the waffle cones. After mixing
the batter and pressing the iron, Meryl
sat quietly for seven minutes, reading
comics until the cones cooled enough for
kids to hold.

When Meryl was younger and people asked her who she
wanted to be when she grew up, she said a doctor, a teacher,
or a tightrope walker.

Bear's favorite ice cream is vanilla with
sandwich cookie pieces. Whenever he
and Meryl are in the same room, they
talk about that. Sometimes she brings
him a little carton from the shop. It's
made fresh that day.

Tiny is sixteen, and Kelley is still seven years older. When Kelley was eighteen, Tiny's dad told him he needed to go to college or to the war about gas. It was a big fight. Tiny didn't understand why Kelley couldn't stay at home anymore. It seemed okay before. She heard everything through a floor vent. It doesn't make sense, how giant, life-changing conversations can happen in fifteen minutes. Next morning was awful. Tiny knew, she knew her dad or Kelley could say they were sorry. They were scared. Please stay. But neither one did, and so Kelley made plans to go.

That afternoon he folded some socks and t-shirts and a green and gold book into a duffel. He bought a bus ticket to the city where people get ready to fly to war. Kelley didn't tell Meryl, so Tiny had to. Meryl decided Kelley was too brokenhearted to tell her himself, and Tiny didn't argue. When Tiny remembers this time, it's like her whole chest has freezer burn. She feels it substernally.

When he left, Meryl stick-and-poked a K on her own wrist, in the same spot where Kelley's X is. When Kelley came back nine months later, they met to sit on a bench. Meryl said she had been waiting for him this whole time, and Kelley said that was strange. He hadn't been waiting for her. They hadn't even talked about anything. Later, they had sex. Tiny heard that through the floor vent too. Since then Kelley and Meryl only sleep with each other, and Kelley lives in his old bedroom again. Tiny made a space for his deodorant in the bathroom again, and that was it. Kelley will tell her everything when he's ready.

Now Kelley is a ghost. He is like Meryl used to be when she looked at him, only now Kelley is that all the time. His brain is all sky. Tiny doesn't have words for what Kelley saw in the war, which is sort of her fault but not in a bad way. When she imagines what Kelley saw, Tiny sees angry washes of color. Sounds like teeth, blood, and bingo chips. Tiny is actually not interested in specifically imagining war, because what comes next are reasons for weapons, and using weapons, and all of that being okay. It is never okay, and she will never change her mind, so she is not interested in the map of it either. Tiny couldn't hear it if she tried. She is stubborn, but not unreasonable. Bear says Tiny is lucky she has never seen true evil. When she was young, he wanted her to be grateful about that. Now he means it hopefully, which is also an avoidance.

Meryl has jewel caves of patience for Kelley's stories. His anecdotal deaths. The magazines call them necrometrics. Little girls, like Tiny and Izzy were, wearing plastic sheets, peeling crabby skin and cobweb bandages. Grown women on their backs in the road, bodies spilling through their shoulders. Hands on the ground. Blood. Space that was people. No sound, and every one at once. Because Meryl listens to these stories, Kelley starts to love her back. He loves her hard. They lie in bed together. Holding each other together. Reminding each other. Eventually, they are home all the time, so Tiny stops listening through the floor vent.

Tiny is not angry with her mother for dying, Bear for living, or her father for sending Kelley to war. She understands there was no other way to do it. She knows that their bodies are in hers. Are hers. If her father didn't want her to be a girl, she might have gone to war instead of Kelley. Then it could be Kelley who was left. He would be the lonely one.

Tiny and Izzy's favorite part about dancing is being in the dark. In the dark, everyone is together and separate. When they need to talk, Tiny and Izzy slide one hand along the other's ribs. Once Tiny sweated so much she soaked through her hair. It felt longer and heavier, like something landed on it. A bird.

In the dark, Tiny and Izzy hold hands. Or Izzy puts her face in Tiny's back, her arms around her stomach. They make one gentle monster. It reverses when they were little and Izzy wanted her back cracked. Tiny always remembers she is a little older. She always looks out for Izzy, except during special songs. Then Tiny locks her knees and dances by herself. When it's over, they walk outside and usually Hank is there, too, watching the sun rise. It gilds and gently warms everyone's face, and the air around them all is soft.

Before Kelley died, Meryl taught Tiny to ride a bike. At first Tiny was scared. She gripped the handlebars so tightly little red mouths opened on her knuckles. Eventually Tiny rode to the corner, and the next corner, and then the corner store, where she and Meryl celebrated with dreamsicles.

Now, Tiny rides to remember there are muscles and blood in her body. This is a good memory. She hasn't crystallized. No dirt piled on her head. When she dismounts back at the house, sometimes Tiny sees her heart. She sees her blood in her wrists like hummingbird wings. She sees her hands flying away. They do not belong to her anyway. They are on a mission.

Early spring mornings are gentle and bright, with corkscrew hazel interrupting Tiny's peripheral vision in chocolate and gold, and blue-purple lungwort in bloom. Tiny closes her eyes on easy turns. As she loops, Tiny makes good intentions for everyone in her family who still has a body. She includes Meryl and Hank, and Izzy, and Aunt Charlotte, and her father. Without him, Tiny is not here at all.

After ARMS was happening awhile, the event moved from Thuy's family restaurant to the old artificial limb store. It hadn't sold limbs for months, but there were still papers and plastic in the corners. Most of the equipment had been picked through, especially the steel parts or anything small and light, like fake fingers. Tiny didn't understand fake fingers. If you have fingers, they're your fingers. None of it is fake.

The equipment that was still there was heavy, and so it was hard to imagine it making anyone's life easier. There were ripped boxes, dusty instructions, and mice prints. Tiny and Izzy imagined their legs gone. Do you still feel your feet? They weren't sure. It is important to imagine rough situations and different bodies, specifically, even when there is no definitive answer. It feels different, depending on who you are. Tiny and Izzy did not imagine white people coming here to buy these limbs, because the limbs did not look realistic, and all the colors were terrible.

People said that when the artificial limb store owner divorced, he sold the shop to a developer. But the developer couldn't find anyone who wanted to build apartment buildings or a fusion concept restaurant, so the place sat empty until Thuy, Shawn, and Marnie asked if they could use it on Saturdays. They received a three-month discount in exchange for cleaning everything first. They lugged in Shawn's auntie's old speakers, sprayed the door day-glo, and pried binary gender signs off the restroom doors. They charged six dollars at the door for cleaning, snacks, decorations, and the community.

Once UP IN ARMS had its own space, more people came, especially ones who had been uncomfortable saying hello to families before dancing all night. Tiny and Izzy always thought that was silly. They were dancing in someone's home. Say hi. Keep walking if you want.

Sometimes part of Tiny wants to cry, and a part doesn't. When this happens, her jaw aches. Sometimes she walks around the produce section at the grocery store, weighing potatoes and rubbing underneath her ears. Tiny doesn't care if people think she's unanchored. She is. Grief unanchors you. Her body is lost in time. She breathes, and usually it passes, but sometimes Tiny can't stop crying. That happens randomly, like when she sees a plastic cracker packet in the gutter. Red and yellow. Kelley ate those all the time. Aunt Charlotte would say this was him sending a message, and maybe Aunt Charlotte is right. But it's also a reminder that bodies are everywhere. Paths are everywhere. Part of Tiny doesn't understand why people still make those cracker packets if Kelley can't eat them anymore. She is angry with the world for continuing, and angry with herself for being angry.

Aunt Charlotte says that when you want to cry but shouldn't, you touch the tip of your tongue to the roof of your mouth, right behind your teeth, and look towards the ceiling. This freezes your face so it can't cry. Tiny uses this tip, but sometimes it makes her gag.

Tiny likes walking in the mornings, so she does it every day. The very early mornings are like walking on a far-away misty planet, but Tiny is still Tiny. Alarms can be rude, in dreams, so Tiny asks the birds to wake her up. She sees them in flashes and wings, Ms and Vs in the air. Tiny's favorites are soft with brown breasts. She would like to be someone who recognizes all the bird songs, but she isn't yet. Maybe her mother was. Tiny hates not being able to ask. Actually, she could ask, but maybe no one would know. Sometimes Tiny imagines writing her mother a letter and mailing it. It would not be totally surprising to receive a letter back. Tiny might not recognize the handwriting, but she likes thinking she would. She likes thinking it wouldn't even be a problem. Hi, Mom.

When it's still too dark to see her hand in front of her face, Tiny imagines walking through a rainbow. In her mind she lightens everything, including birds, from purple to indigo to green as other people wake up. At noon, everything is gently red. Tiny's favorite part is early purple, when everything is new-bruise color and she can start to see shadows. Sometimes Tiny hears a hum, which means more people are leaving their dreams. People are waking up or turning over, playing music and splashing water on their faces. More and more people awake means more light. Noon isn't scary, but it's loud.

Tiny keeps her old dirt-beat shoes by the bed, so when she hears the birds she can just go. Instead of brushing her teeth, Tiny just starts walking on the sidewalks, then through fields and finally, the forest. She pretends it is all ocean. At first Tiny's eyes have crusts in them. She walks, and she imagines her head and nose heating first. Next, her shoulders and chest. Creatures curving around her. Everything is ocean. Everything is alive. Tiny knows she's never the only one.

Kelley is dead, and Tiny kept one of his shirts. The really old lime one. It's a perfect day. It makes people forget who they are. Tiny wears it instead of emptying the dishwasher, because when she used to empty the dishwasher, Kelley would be in the other room. There is a hair grease stain inside the collar. Whenever Tiny wears the shirt, she measures her own hair against that stain. When her hair grows longer than the stain, which has to happen eventually, because Tiny is not dead, she tells a stranger a story about Kelley. She tells them a joke, or boosts their confidence like Kelley would. This too is how Tiny stays alive, for now.

The stain is smooth on top and scalloped on the bottom, like something came out of Kelley's neck teeth first. Like a worm. Like they had to tunnel out. When Tiny thinks about the worm, she imagines Kelley laughing at her, and then she doesn't want to cry. She remembers how Kelley's laugh sounds. When even that doesn't work, for example when Kelley's favorite sports teams finally win, and the crowd hugs and screams, Tiny starts to cry because Kelley isn't here to celebrate with her. Kelley was no Fairweather Johnson. He always knew this day would come, meaning the day their team would win, and now it has but he isn't. When Tiny starts to cry and can't stop, she visits water, because crying in front of water feels whole. It reintroduces old friends. Tiny goes alone. We are all hairy bags of water anyway.

Loss is connected to love because without the one, the other means nothing at all. This is not a threat. It is a fact about the state of the universe.

When Tiny and Hank fell in love, she tried on his pants and realized they had the same size hips.

When Tiny and Hank fell in love, they gave each other bouquets of mimosa and mint.

They wore mood rings on their pinkie fingers, until they went ice skating and froze both rings on a muddy color.

They walked through the drive-through and bought strawberry malts, extra malt, and ate them in the parking lot with spoons.

When Tiny and Hank fell in love, Izzy took a picture of them looking at her and saw they loved her too.

When Tiny and Hank fell in love, Tiny still turned off her phone when she slept at Izzy's house. She kept waking up to walk alone in the mornings.

When Tiny and Hank fell in love, they biked through cherry blossoms. They biked through yellow leaves.

When Tiny and Hank fell in love, she knitted him a snowdrop olive green hat and he wore it all the time, in almost every season.

When Tiny and Hank fell in love, he cooked pots of rice and garlic and chicken broth when she was sick.

They fell asleep thigh to thigh, holding each other in one small bed.

They sat in the middle seats at movies, and by the windows on the bus.

When Tiny and Hank fell in love, they watched home videos of tornadoes on the internet. They watched people mixing paint.

When Tiny and Hank fell in love, the first person who woke up smiled quietly at the ceiling.

When Tiny and Hank fell in love, Tiny realized she liked falling asleep holding people who weren't Izzy or her self.

When Tiny and Hank fell in love, they went to basketball games at the local college. They sat high up, because those seats were cheap, and they could watch games like a pattern unfolding. They named the patterns together.

In the mornings as she walks, Tiny counts layers of dirt, pawprints, and blown seeds, and so the back of her neck gets burned. Bear never says use aloe. He doesn't know to say it. Bear is edged in grief, like Tiny is. Like piping on a pastry. The rules Bear makes now, in grief, must be to protect someone else. Someone who isn't Tiny. Another child, or a memory of one, or maybe even himself, because his rules don't make Tiny feel safe at all. In fact, Bear's rules make it hard to breathe. Hard to be. But Tiny tries, because after all Bear is still her father. His body made hers, and so her body is part of his, and so when Tiny goes out into the fields, she carries her father with her. She is her father. His rules and examples help them both, like when Tiny doesn't fall out of trees, or when the sun wakes her up and she is ready to go. Like when Tiny dives into love. Sometimes though, she is just a doom.

Tiny is building an altar in the woods, in the crook of a baldhip rose, which she likes because it has fruit and thorns and lives brightly through the winter. There is a pink candle with glitter pressed into it in pentagrams, and the meteorite necklace from Hank, which looks better on branches than necks. Hank doesn't care that he never sees it on her. Gifts don't come with rules. Hanging from another branch is one of Izzy's baby shoes, a soft pink with stubbed toes. It holds a zirconium stud found in the frozen aisle of Fresh Taste Foods, purple beads from a poet wobbly on mezcal, a hamburger wrapper cold-wiped clean of cheese, and a half-full bottle of lavender oil. Also in the tree are pieces of brown eggshell, a sticky hand from the laundromat machine, and a sticky note Tiny found in a book. Her mother's handwriting is on it, probably. Tiny isn't sure.

And the crows bring gifts. They leave small pieces of machinery and lawn furniture, and buttons, and sometimes a small dead animal to cure. The altar gets bigger and bigger, and some mornings Tiny can tell squirrels slept there too. Sometimes she leaves out bread and popcorn. All altars could also be plates and beds. In a dream Tiny threw the whole tree into a cave, and when she came back a day later, it was all studded with crystals. It was a galaxy growing. This little altar makes Tiny's mornings into a pilgrimage. When she sees the candle's pink through the trees, she knows it's almost time to turn around and go home.

First she sees the pink and walks towards it, and when Tiny reaches the rose, she stretches her arms wide and throws back her head. Takes one huge breath. Says hello. Sometimes Tiny sits on the ground with one hand on the moss. The green is so flushed it makes her hand look like a ghost's.

COMMITTED SUICIDE implies a crime.

The root of CRIME is unclear.

Some people think it's a decision.
A sifting.

Some people say it's a cry of distress,
or for help. It isn't about trying,
but asking and asking,

and no could hear.

At that point, intent doesn't matter.
You are saying: I need this to be alive.

I need this to stay.

Giving into mourning feels like going over a waterfall in a barrel. Or without a barrel. At night Tiny looks up pictures of waterfalls on the internet. Sometimes this is freeing. You are mourning. You are going over a waterfall in a barrel.

Tiny remembers the first time Kelley disappeared. It was around four o'clock in the wintertime, so the air outside was light gray. Kelley wore two sweatshirts at once, and he didn't come back for three days. When he did, Kelley hadn't shaved. He looked tired. Until she heard his car driving back into the garage, Tiny had been frightened. Still, she hadn't called Meryl, because maybe Kelley and Meryl were together, and if they weren't, then why worry Meryl. Kelley came back late at night. Tiny heard his feet on the stairs and saw the bathroom light appear underneath her door. Kelley flicked the on switch so carefully Tiny heard the electricity hum. In the morning, there was a slightly crushed dandelion outside her door, its stem milky and tightly-squeezed. Hello. I'm back. Here we are.

Then, Kelley kept leaving. He never went very far, but he never stayed home very long either. It was a restlessness like Tiny's, except it didn't come naturally to Kelley. He couldn't tell her it was okay or going to be okay. Whenever he came back, Kelley's cheekbones looked sharper. Still, they were beautiful. His cheekbones. Once Izzy practiced makeup on Kelley, and he looked like a movie star. Like he could sell cars, musical instruments, or refrigerators. Kelley could convince someone to do something important, even something involving love. Tiny keeps all the pictures she ever took of Kelley in a drawer by her bed, and sometimes she looks at them. When Tiny takes the picture, Kelley smiles like Bear used to smile.

In the beginning, Kelley always left something for Tiny outside her bedroom door. She would lie awake listening for the drop, for the rustle of a wrapper or the scratch of wild garlic. Once she heard it, she could sleep.

Kelley left a cassette with juke on it.

He left three circles of charcoal.

A tracing of his hand on a Korean restaurant menu.

A yellow rubber band that said SUNSHINE.

Towards the end Tiny simply wouldn't look down, in case Kelley hadn't come home at all. For her, this was penance and vigilance.

If Tiny didn't look down, Kelley might just be in the other room. She would see him.

One night Bear and Kelley had a fight. You should be happy, said Bear. You can go to college. You have a beautiful girlfriend. You pulled yourself out of that mud. He spat mud like a stone. Bear was trying so hard to be a good dad, but it wasn't working for anyone. Dad, said Kelley, Dad. You didn't — then Tiny climbed out on the roof, and she didn't listen to anything else.

It is violent not to say the cause of death, even when there isn't one.

It is violent because we imagine everything, or nothing.

It is violent because it comes after.

We never thought we'd be here. We never wanted this.

Books with happy endings frighten Tiny.
Originally, comedy meant: it ends with a wedding.

Happiness is always possible, but depending on who you are,
some kinds of happy endings are not realistic, they are selfish,
and also, they are boring.

Tiny's mother always said: we don't say boring in our family.

Listen to me: you can survive this period.

I hope you suffer little additional violence.

I hope you allow yourself to exist in space and time.

I hope the breaks in your heart help you to see.

Tiny hates when people say she is in high school. She is not in anything but her body. She does not belong to anyone but herself. When she was little, Tiny peeled off the scab before it was ready. She felt pain as noise, and then it was gone. Tiny has only ever slept with two people. Falling asleep on the same pillow is holy, she thinks. The cells must drift. The dreams.

Tiny's greatest fear in the world is dying alone, but now she knows she won't. It is scientifically impossible. Part of loving someone is sharing bodies, which then become one big body. Or maybe, many different bodies that hold similar facts about the world. The world in time. Tiny isn't sure.

When she can't sleep, she puts one hand on her heart. Tiny feels her heart, which is a muscle, moving closer to her palm, then away. Tiny is not attached to anything beyond this rhythm, which is time now kept by Hank and Izzy too. Here we all are, all the time.

Some Saturdays, once everything at the new UP IN ARMS had been cleaned and re-cleaned, Marnie brings Violet, her six-year-old daughter. Violet likes to dance butt-first. She likes to hug Shawn's leg and sit on his foot. Marnie set up a bed for Violet in the old manager's office, with a pillow from home and flannels from the lost and found and a little hot pink glitter. Violet dances for the first hour, and then she sleeps in the office. Marnie checks in regularly. Sometimes she naps too. Sleeping during noise is power. So is making places to be free. While Violet sleeps, Izzy and Tiny dance the one-arm dance. Tiny runs outside to borrow Hank's hat, and then he is dancing too. The air is around them all, and the light and the sound and no one knows what time it is. No one knows if it's morning yet, but they're not worried about it.

Izzy still thinks Thuy is incredibly beautiful. It is a beauty Izzy doesn't know how to describe. She doesn't want to be Thuy, and seeing Thuy always makes Izzy nervous. It makes her feel like her feet are safe in two separate apartment complexes. Izzy could watch Thuy dance forever.

After three weeks, thinking about talking to Thuy still makes Izzy want to evaporate, but then she asks a question anyway. Izzy asks about the weather. It is a thirty-second conversation, but she is trying. Tiny and Hank are proud.

Two weeks later, Thuy gives Tiny and Izzy one green bottle of beer apiece and they dance an extra hour, clapping on the twos, the three of them alone while the sun comes up pink.

They don't say very much, just dance without bones from their chests to their knees.

They dance to music many other people have danced to too.

At the end, Thuy, Tiny, and Izzy sit outside against the building, to relax and watch the sun.

Some nights the tamale guy walks into UP IN ARMS with his busted red cooler. He sells three tamales, wrapped in foil and tucked into plastic, for three dollars. Tiny and Izzy buy a bag and eat two right away, which burns their tongues. They split the third, swallow quickly, and get back to dancing.

When Tiny was in her goth lipstick phase she'd smear black on the husks. Izzy thought it looked tough.

Last night's last song was:
SHINE   THE   LIGHT   ON   THE   FOLKS,   HONEY
YOU ARE MY FRIEND MY FRIEND

Tiny's first death was her mother. Her second was Laura, a girl Tiny knew since kindergarten. One day in seventh grade, Laura fell out of her desk and lay shaking on the floor. A stream of blood slid out her nose, thick as an adult's thumb. The stream became wider than Laura's nostril. The teacher found a spoon and put it in Laura's mouth, gently, to press down her tongue. Tiny thought about steel on tastebuds. How Laura would probably wake up with a skull throb. She never thought Laura wouldn't wake up at all.

When Laura did wake up, she was scared because she was on the floor. The teacher helped her sit up and drink a box of fruit punch. Laura's eyes looked bubbled, like the thermometer of her had scrambled. The class stopped talking about pyramids and took a spontaneous recess. Since Izzy was in the other seventh grade section, Tiny sat alone and worked on the friendship bracelet she'd pinned to the knee of her jeans. It was a skinny chain, with a skinnier chain running around the outside, a swirled playground slide in hot pink, yellow, and acid green. Tiny knotted and knotted and looked up at the crows. They were watching her too.

Laura had three more seizures in class. The last one was big. Everyone heard a crack when her head hit the floor, but this time there wasn't any blood. The blood must be on the inside, thought Tiny. She was frightened by a body losing itself. By a body that was usually Laura becoming a foaming floppy sack, and the fog in Laura's eyes when she came back to herself. Tiny hated the idea of coming back to herself. What if Laura talked to other people while she seized? What if it was her portal to other planets? Tiny knew that probably wasn't true, but the idea helped her with the unanswerable question, which was: where did Laura go? She seemed calmer afterwards. Maybe the other side was more comfortable, or simply different.

After the last very bad one, Laura stopped coming to class, and then there was a long year when she was in the hospital all the time. Tiny didn't know how much it cost. She told Izzy: if we get older, never let anyone do that to me. Tiny does not want to sit in a white metal bed with tubes in her veins and urethra. With her body turning to passive sponge. Izzy said, okay. But. If I don't let people do that to you, you'll die. You'll leave me. Someday, said Tiny. Obviously. For a while. Okay, said Izzy, but if you get sick in the hospital before you're ninety-five, I need you to let doctors help. Ninety, said Tiny. Okay, Izzy said. That's a long time from now, you know.

Laura never came back to school, but Tiny visited her once. She didn't tell Hank or Izzy, and she took the bus forty minutes each way. Tiny brought a palm-sized cup of lime pudding and some whiskery chrysanthemums. When the nurse left to find a vase, Tiny pulled out a piece of her own hair, whispered hi into Laura's ear, and then left the hair on the pillow so Laura would not be alone. It did not occur to Tiny, who already lived with death, that she was not responsible for Laura's illness, or her feelings about the hospital, which in fact Tiny could not know. Finally, she slipped her hand underneath one of Laura's, palm to palm.

Now there was nothing pressuring anyone from flying away. Everyone could float, when it was time. The girls never saw each other again, but on the way out of Laura's room, Tiny opened her mouth and imagined crows screaming out over everyone. She imagined them, and she saw them. They weren't angry. They were crows. We're here, they said. We're here, we're here. So are you.

When she saw Kelley's body, Tiny's hearing left hers. Suddenly she really was a boat, only not in a safe way. She was out, far out underneath an angry green sky. The kind of sky that means earthquake. Tiny didn't trust sounds anymore, and the ones she did hear made her dizzy. Bird songs were screws twisting into hard wood, and dogs sounded like air conditioners. Pulling shoelaces sounded like ice cracking. This lasted a week. On the last day of it, walking in the forest, Tiny was sure she heard a moldy hunk of cedar chirping. That night, Tiny fell asleep with both hands on her heart. In the morning, her vertigo was gone. The day after that, she could hear like before.

One Saturday Tiny had terrible cramps. Thuy gave her aspirin, but it didn't help. It was a dull, clenched pain, turning sharp on a beat. Tiny lay on the floor with her head in Izzy's lap. She took off her shoes. Izzy stroked Tiny's hair. They waited together. Two bodies in time. Tiny almost never feels physical pain, but when she does it is a heavy blanket over her whole body. It makes her hot, crabby, and fuzzy-brained. After a while, Tiny was okay to walk, and so, arms around waists, she and Izzy went home.

While they waited for the bus, Tiny's head on Izzy's shoulder, this guy pulled up his car. Izzy's throat twisted when she saw him watching with one hand. She wished she hadn't left her brass knuckles at home. Tiny wished she hadn't learned to be angry at people who pulled over in their cars. Neither wish changed the man. It was clear he wasn't trying to help.

Tiny lifted her head, flashed her eyes, mouthed get off. We're fine. Suddenly the bus was coming, so the man drove away. On the bus, Izzy said she wished she could fix Tiny's pain. Her cramps, and her heart. It makes you different, Izzy said. I wish I could take everything away. She started to cry. Don't, said Tiny. This is how it gets better. You know how strong we are. I know, said Izzy, and took a big sniffy breath that filled her chest. The bus kept moving, and the streetlights dappled everyone's face.

Tiny: I read about medicines for cancer. One loosens all the hair from your body. A wet eraser across a cloudy chalkboard. All the memory of hair is gone.

Sound depends on hair. If you lose your hair, your hearing changes as well.

If I ever get sick like Mom—which I might, my body was her body and trauma lurks, it is inherited—

Izzy: Tiny. Maybe, but you aren't sick right now.

When Tiny and I listen to music in bed, we put one bud in her left ear and one in my right. Sometimes Tiny falls asleep immediately, so I turn off the music and feel her heart beating instead.

One Saturday a man saw the book Izzy was reading, which had a glove on the cover. He asked her why she read about gloves. Well there is this one part, said Izzy, where the girl loses her glove in a train station. And trains are zooming back and forth on both sides. The people change and the light changes, and the smells change, but the glove stays the same. Does she find it again? the man asked, and Izzy said that wasn't the point. It's beautiful to think about. It isn't a real glove. She doesn't need it for warmth or protection.

Next, the man leaned into Izzy's face. His hair smelled like green apples, and he kissed her on the cheek. Beautiful, he said. The kiss smacked, and the man left part of his sweat mustache. At first Izzy was confused, and then she was angry. But the man left right away. He hadn't written her a better ending. Hadn't tried to explain a book he never read. So Izzy felt a little sweet about it, secretly. She took it as a compliment. She never told Tiny, who would have found the man and yelled at him.

WHEN WILL YOU LEARN

TO BE

IN THIS WORLD?

Sometimes Hank danced with Tiny and Izzy, or sometimes he sat outside.

Sometimes he didn't come out at all. Hank had other phases and interests.

For a while, Hank was into stand-up comedy. His Uncle Ray showed him an internet video of a man singing I Trusted You, I Trusted You, I Trusted You for over eight minutes. As the song continued, the man became angrier and angrier, and the crowd started shrinking back like he was poison ivy. Hank loved the intensity. This man wasn't messing around, and when the song finished, he left the stage.

After that, Hank was into horror movie makeup. Once when Hank left the house because his parents were fighting, he walked to the used bookstore and read about how vampires and phantoms would tape their noses up and their ears back. For a while Hank went to UP IN ARMS with his ears taped back too. Eventually, Izzy told him people didn't understand the tribute.

Once Hank bought one thousand glow-in-the-dark star stickers, snuck into Tiny's bedroom, and arranged them in a scientifically accurate map over her bed. In space, Hank learned, there is no air, and so there is no sound. Tiny thought it was hilarious, and very sweet, but then she took them down so the room could be dark again.

Bear believes in the law. One happy ending for everyone, rooted in the law. He believes that if this ending does not make you happy, you must be sick. There must be damage. And that isn't wrong, because many things that make Bear happy make other people happy too. Bear does not wish disease on anyone. Above all, he wants to keep the people he loves safe and happy. He trusts the system, and it trusts him. An infinity symbol.

Tiny believes in asking people what they like and want. If their response is completely new to her, fine. She can learn about it. She can weigh the risks. Like Bear, Tiny wants safety, but they see it differently. When Tiny thinks about her life, she sees an ocean apart from time. The future she wants is not here yet. It might not come before she dies. That doesn't mean it's wrong.

Everything Bear does is connected to the war, which is connected to capitalism and the prison industry and cis white men and power and quirky little touches, like striped socks to show logical flexibility. Everything Tiny does is allowed to desire, to want or to grow wild, which is hard to write about because it is always changing. In fact, it must change to stay relevant. This is inconvenient for everyone, including Tiny. She seems selfish, naïve, and impatient a lot of the time, and then she is angry because she doesn't want to be any of that. She is, after all, still young.

Izzy tells Tiny that the only thing suicide is for sure is deliberate. It is a decision. It is opening your mouth and screaming. This is ordinary, and it is scary. Death happens every day. It always leaves people. Inside the chrysalis, caterpillars melt almost completely before becoming butterflies, and afterwards, they remember flashes of their earlier life. Izzy says it's like remembering a bassline, Tiny. Dance is memory. Mouths and wounds are soft and red. Exits and entrances.

Izzy doesn't think suicide is selfish, even if the dictionary says it must be. She and Tiny know bodies echo. They shimmer. For example, sometimes Shawn gets called in to his other job, so Marnie takes his ARMS shift. She always starts with one of Shawn's mixes. That music is. It is in the air. It started in Shawn's body, and now it is in Izzy and Tiny's too. Everyone dances in space. Mourning is separate. It is vocal and cloth.

Bodies continue imperfectly, like the weather. Kelley is gone, but also he isn't. Sometimes Tiny dreams she is Kelley instead. She dreams her mother is here.

I saw him, says Tiny. I saw him and I still see him. I think forwards, and he's gone.

Have you cried about that yet? asks Izzy. Not yet, says Tiny. At least, I don't think so.

What if I can't stop? Then you won't, Izzy shrugs. We'll figure it out.

Hank is always anxious, which is why he likes to smoke. When Hank smokes, he can understand calm. Otherwise, he doesn't. Tiny processes the situation like looking out a window. If the road sparkles, it's raining. If Hank's smoking, he's calm. Everyone else pressures Hank to feel more confident, which isn't necessarily the wrong end goal. But Hank wants a recipe. He needs a map. To make lemon bars, you need lemons, olive oil, and shortbread. Eventually, you have lemon bars. Eventually, you will have confidence. Hank feels like sometimes his lemon bars turn into lug nuts or mice. When Hank feels this way, Tiny runs a finger from the inside of his wrist to his armpit and back, slowly.

This isn't forever, she says. We're all learning.

I love you as much as a human heart can, says Tiny. I love you too, says Hank. They know the world changes. They know they will love each other, even when they can't explain every single part of the rest. You're home to me, says Tiny, and Hank says yeah.

At Kelley's funeral, which is not in a veteran cemetery, everyone tells Meryl she will move past this. Like death is a road sign. They don't mean it unkindly, they mean: you're young. They say they are so sorry. It's a shame about the war. Like the war could end. Like it could be separated from all other parts of life. Like Kelley can be forgotten in Meryl's. In theirs, which is now a diagnosis. A cliff. People Meryl won't remember offer to bring her casseroles and amusement park passes, and she makes her mouth smile. Her eyes are out of light.

When Meryl sees Kelley in the casket, he is still Kelley, and Meryl wants to climb in. She wants to hold his hand, even if it feels like a water bed. She leans in to kiss Kelley's neck, and it smells like ice, chemicals, and hair gel. After that he is gone for ever. Meryl hallucinates the casket filling with smoke. It is dotted through with seed pearls and floating clumps of hair. Meryl wonders if anyone else sees the smoke. She imagines filling her pockets with it. Now the casket is closed.

When Hank and Tiny have sex it is almost always in Tiny's bedroom. They have sex like it could fill their pockets. Afterwards, almost always, they eat oranges, even when oranges aren't in season. The carbon footprint is a luxury and a waste, and so sometimes, afterwards, alone, Hank donates money to the ocean on the internet.

Tiny doesn't like sharing her orange, but whenever she peels it in one unbroken spiral, she drapes the strip across Hank's chest before they set an alarm and sleep for twenty-five minutes. For the rest of the day, Tiny smells her wrists and imagines Hank and oranges are with her, because they are. To Tiny, this is love. It is a room where she could be, live, and stay.

After the funeral, people sit in a room with ash-veined floors and heavy vases jammed full of iceberg roses with pale yellow centers. They eat food Bear chose. Pucker-salted capers, eggs deviled with lemon juice and Dijon, chocolate cake cut into triangles, and an entire platter of pears dying in foil.

Tiny eats corn chips spitefully, by the fistful. They look like curled ears. She bites down slowly, waiting for the chili to fan out on her tongue. It keeps her awake. She isn't tired. Tiny understands that it is important to be here now too, for Bear. For him to hug her into his armpit like she is a life jacket. It is exhausting as well. Tiny is exhausted by Kelley's decision. By his relief, and by the future. No one knows what questions to ask. Everyone talks endlessly about the temperature. About Kelley when he was a baby. Tiny wants to talk about Kelley last winter, when he turned into a ghost, but she doesn't know how to start. She also wants to peel off her skin, or sob. Her face is calm. She relaxes her mouth.

Tiny remembers shopping with someone, her mother or Aunt Charlotte, and asking permission to walk into the center of a round clothing rack. The adult said yes, as a special treat, and Tiny chose a display of mesh jerseys vibrating from pink to blood. She wanted to fall asleep in there, like she wants to fall asleep now under the deviled egg table. Let someone else take care awhile. The problem is that at this point, there is no one else for the job. Tiny must fill it, and so she will.

After ninety minutes, the only people left in the room are Bear and Tiny, and people Bear works with and people who fought in the war. One man read a poem about a thunderstorm with lightning-legs. The rain was a shaggy belly dragging over the fields.

The room is full of people with muscles and pressed clothing and appropriateness. People who understand before and after, because they lived it too. Tiny wants to give everyone a present. She wants to give them cars, yards, and families, because these are things they want. Like Bear, Tiny wants everyone to be safe and happy.

She looks out the window and sees Meryl, Izzy, and Hank sitting in the trunk of Kelley's friend's hatchback. They nip a handle of whiskey, and Tiny realizes why they're called handles. Because they have handles. Meryl's shoulders are oceaning, and Izzy is rubbing her back. Hank looks like he doesn't know what to say, and so Tiny is proud he's staying.

If Kelley were here, he would walk with Tiny from this room with its sick-pale roses and monochromatic clothing. They would walk out to the parking lot. They would talk with everyone in the room and everyone in the car, and it would make a whole. Only Kelley's body is meat, now. It is turning into something else.

Finally Tiny feels the cracks, and she starts to cry. It's a relief. A man with a birthmark the shape and color of a cremini mushroom hands her a pack of tissues. Your father loves you so much, he says. I know, says Tiny. I love him too. Thank you.

What if there is no crime?

What if there is a hole, and a different shape around that hole?

These are questions no one can answer yet.

For a long time after Kelley dies, Tiny is obsessed with the pieces people leave out at rituals and in offices.

An obsession is different than a phase. An obsession can involve the brain but not the body. A phase involves everything.

Tiny goes through a phase where she steals these pieces too. Tiny needs to understand. She takes thimbles of sand from incense holders at the meditation temple, retractable-ball pens from veterinary clinics, and loose petals from plastic bouquets at the craft store. None of these pieces ever go into the forest. Tiny hopes that separation will explain something to her.

She wants a map. She wants to be told how to live in this body that now holds two dead people in it. Tiny stares at her face in the mirror and waits for it to change.

Tiny has something to say at the funeral. Bear will listen, but he is nervous. He knows Tiny will speak from her heart, which will make her vulnerable. It might seem like his child doesn't understand sacrifice. Bear imagines his friends looking at Tiny with pity. Pity can be merciful, or it can create even more distance.

When she stands at the ambo, Tiny doesn't register anyone's face. She feels her heart spin like a green jewel. Kelley, she says, was like wildflowers. Not one, but a field. He was beautiful—

—now Tiny stops, and she *does* cry, the past tense makes her cry, she looks into the audience and sees Meryl staring at her. Meryl, who cried out all her liquids. Meryl is also a flower. To center, Tiny pictures wild blooms on her walks through the woods: hissing red bergamot and burst-purple asters, orange marshmallow poppies and the thistles she remembers picking for her mother. They look like violet-flame matches. They are also weeds.

Kelley, says Tiny, was a field of wildflowers: dirty, tangled, and heart-stoppingly beautiful. Half-buried, half-sunning:

> Once we were at the mall, and a
> lady stopped to say: your eyes look
> like planets. They did look like
> planets, says Tiny. They did.

> Now people make noises.

> They're moving around, and Tiny knows
> it's because they're imagining
> Kelley's eyes too. Kelley is here,
> and he is gone.

Tiny looks up again and sees Hank and Izzy sitting together in the very back of the church. Izzy wears a black lace top, and the two of them hold hands while the funeral sits on their chests. Next Tiny tells the story about Kelley's eleventh birthday, when they had pancakes for cake, and everyone made a scarecrow the size of their parents, because they were using their parents' clothes to make them. Tiny talks about falling asleep in the corner of Kelley's bedroom, because it felt safe. She doesn't mention the body or the war. She wants to say: you could have fixed this.

But she doesn't, because it wouldn't be true. No one could have. It is a web. We are a web. Without the war, Bear wouldn't be Bear. Without the war, Kelley would probably be alive. But he isn't. As she walks back to the pews, Tiny is surprised her hair doesn't float into the air.

For two weeks after the funeral, Tiny can't visit her altar in
the woods. She sort of forgets about it. There was a funeral,
Tiny keeps thinking. A funeral. My brother is dead. Brother
dead funeral Kelley. Some days, Tiny's brain says that over
and over, like a song they'd play at UP IN ARMS when it was
time for everyone to go to work or sleep.

Tiny imagines cutting down the forest instead. Carving
its trees into a giant KELLEY. Setting his name on fire. She
imagines the charred grass and the soot-smeared concrete.

It would be huge, which wouldn't change anything.

Actually, you could visit the tree, says Izzy. She hasn't seen Tiny's altar, but she knows it exists. Just walk there. It's not like your legs fell off. Duh, Tiny says. She stretches them out in front of her. One has a spider bite. Izzy tries a different way. Don't you want to see how things are changing over there? I don't, Tiny replies. Time doesn't work for me right now, and I'm mad it does for other people. Tiny, says Izzy, why are you mad at a tree?

 Tiny thinks about her spider bite. A spider must have crawled onto her leg, bitten her, and then crawled off to be a spider. She didn't feel any of it. It didn't even itch, just hardened into an angry crown. The bite makes her think about Meryl. Tiny and Meryl used to have whole futures in common. Now they have a past. A crater. Tiny doesn't know words for any feelings she might have about it. She doesn't know what that future was. It never had a shape. She will see Meryl again, but it won't be the same.

Tiny remembers a story she read in fifth grade about a gorilla who saw a picture of a skeleton. One of the gorilla's human friends asked if the bones were alive or dead. Dead, signed the gorilla. Draped. The human friend asked the gorilla where animals go, and the gorilla said a comfortable hole. Goodbye. Tiny can imagine this hole. It is also a musical. This hole, the charred grass, and the smeared concrete can't change in space. They just are. They exist. But now Tiny can remember imagining them and not-imagining them, which is a start. Mourning is like burying your head in a bucket of mud, and staying there while it seeps into your ears. You drown too, and you don't. One day the bucket is different.

Sometimes Tiny looks in the mirror and thinks:
I'm going to die.

I could do it now.

Tiny, says Bear, are you happy? Tiny says she's okay, but it's hard. It's hard for you too Dad, she says, and he says it's hard for all of us.

Tiny imagines Bear is talking about another world, a place where their family can still sit for breakfast. For breakfast, for all of us.

Tiny imagines asking Bear about new people he might love. About hobbies, about his work and how it continues. About the war and what it's like. For now, Tiny needs to save these questions. She and her dad aren't quite ready.

Tiny drinks her coffee and tells Bear she loves him. She does. Tiny leaves so she can come back. She imagines her life as a soldier like Kelley. It is glass and blood and noise. Tiny will never work for a war. Never take money from it.

The ARMS crowd tonight is large, and suddenly, among many hands, Tiny sees Kelley's with the others. The NO GODS tattoo. She sees it for ten seconds, and she starts to cry. It is true, the hand, even though Kelley hated dancing. He's buried. He is also here. It is not cute, in fact it is slightly annoying because Tiny would rather dream about Kelley so she can ask him questions. So she can hear his voice. Yet Kelley is here, and Tiny can know this and believe it without asking herself any other questions. Kelley is here dancing, and so Tiny dances too. The music says

LL, I NEED YOUR LOVE WELL, I NEED YOUR LOVE WELL, I NEED YOUR LC
LL, I NEED YOUR LOVE WELL, I NEED YOUR LOVE WELL, I NEED YOUR LC

After the song Tiny slips outside without telling Izzy or Hank. She walks around the corner to look at the sky and the milk moon. In its fullness she sees a body-sized patch of dandelions, faces up like tiny lions. For a minute she wants to pick them all, but instead Tiny cries some more. She leaves them to be. The tears mix with her lip gloss and make her chin shine. Tiny cries and cries, and then she stretches her chest towards the moon and walks back inside to slow dance with Izzy.

The next day, Tiny isn't carrying anything. She doesn't have anything in her pockets, not even Kelley's program from the funeral. Her head is bare, and as Tiny walks she looks down at the new flowers: balsamroot and lupine, and a whole hill peppered with camas. She forgot about camas. They are themselves. When they bloom, the entire field turns that color. It is real life, not a metaphor.

Tiny remembers a book about trees communicating with each other through roots. They talk with fungus and electrochemicals. Tiny remembers that some trees are almost a thousand years old. Their long-term is her lifetime at least, times eight. They are nests, apartments, museums, public housing, fields, individuals, and populations all at once. Their tones depend on sun, chemicals, creatures, and who's looking. Who is in need. In this way, the trees are helpers. They are here. As they grow, the boundary changes. The airflow changes, and so do the sounds. It fluctuates and protects.

Tiny looks up in time to see the pink candle. It is still there, and so are the crows. She's been away almost six weeks, and in that time the crows brought pennies and hook earrings and squares of foil. There are screws, travel-size toothpaste tubes, and a stack of white salt crackers. There is a wiggly-eyed spider cupcake topper. Everything here is trash, gift, and memory. The crows themselves are mostly gone, for now, but there are two hopping in the clearing to Tiny's left. Their feathers are iridescent, their tails matter-of-fact fans. Tiny doesn't know if they are friends, or related or what, but she lies on the moss and listens. Maybe these same crows saw Kelley before he was buried, walking to Meryl's or somewhere else. Maybe they followed for a while. Tiny wants to call her younger self to say: hey, the crows are still here. They're looking out. Suddenly Tiny feels both dead and new. A burnt orange.

Finally Tiny is hungry, really hungry, and her body is light. Tiny sees herself sitting up, saying goodbye to the two birds, and walking back through the forest to eat breakfast with Aunt Charlotte.

The sun is pink again. Tiny walks home.

SOURCES

PRIMARY

For dancing, thank you Chances Dances in Chicago, and the American Artificial Limb Company and Electric Tea Garden in Seattle. For shapes and the name UP IN ARMS, thank you Edie Fake. For maps and patterns, thank you Viktor van Bramer, Aay Preston-Myint, and especially Aaron Hughes. For Tiny's attention and sense of restoration ecology, thank you Mom (icyh) and Robin Wall Kimmerer.

SECONDARY

Tiny's name comes from Antigone, but also tinsel.
Here are most of the sparkly threads:

"Say it" is from Maria Dahvana Headley's translation of *Beowulf.*

Tiny's sadness on the roof is like David Wojnarowicz's in *Close to the Knives.* "I can't think of anything I am truly afraid of and I'm trying to give something unspeakable words;"

"Stars exist" is from Inger Christensen's *Alphabet,* translated by Susanna Nied.

The drawings in Tiny's mother's lab notebook are from Chapter 3 ("Symbiogenesis and the Lively Arts of Staying with the Trouble") of Donna Haraway's *Staying with the Trouble: Making Kin in the Chthulucene.*

"DESTROY THE BELIEF THAT / INTIMACY MUST BE RESERVED FOR / MONOGAMOUS RELATIONSHIPS" is from Lora Mathis.

The glove in Tiny's dream and Izzy's book is from André Breton's *Nadja*.

The shadow of the house is from "Laura and Brady in the Shadow of Our House" by Abelardo Morell.

"A bloom is not a parade" is from Fanny Howe's "Bewilderment."

"Blue and pink and starry gold" is from Jolie Holland's "All the Morning Birds."

"'Stress,' that vague and now ubiquitous word for myriad forms of assault that come from outside the organism, is a vehicle by which environment is transmuted into biological being" is from Siri Hustvedt's "Suicide and the Drama of Self Consciousness."

"The representation of a real death is an obscenity. We do not die twice" is from André Bazin's "Death Every Afternoon."

Snail mucus facts are from Mark Davies and Janine Blackwell's research at the University of Sunderland.

The Pizza Dance was invented by Angela Vincent in South Bend, Indiana in 2001.

Aunt Charlotte's paintings are like Morris Louis's veil paintings.

The death scientists take inspiration from the McArthur Forest Fire Danger Index, which was developed by A.G. McArthur.

"Yeah something called love / That's like hypnotizing chickens / Well I am just a modern guy" is from Iggy Pop and David Bowie's "Lust for Life."

The song Tiny sings is "The World's a Mess, It's In My Kiss," by John Doe and Exene Cervenka.

"Keep me safe. Set me free" is from JB Brager's "Protection from Codependency."

The ARMS rules are from Chances Dances, "a night life collective dedicated to holding safer spaces for queer people and building platforms for emerging performers, artists, and musicians" in Chicago, Illinois from 2005-2018. "All Chances parties recognize the power of consent, welcome all gender expressions, and feature gender neutral bathrooms."

"A desire for a more normal life does not necessarily mean identification with norms, but can be simply this: a desire to escape the exhaustion of having to insist just to exist" is from Sara Ahmed's *Willful Subjects*.

"Are you a girl or boy? / Are you a boy or girl?" is from Le Tigre's "On Guard," sung by JD Samson.

In *Hedwig and the Angry Inch*, written by John Cameron Mitchell, Hedwig's mom says, "To be free, one must give up a little part of oneself."

"One of the things one risks when one talks of ghosts is the charge of ignoring the living, the real, and the material" is from José Esteban Muñoz's *Cruising Utopia*.

"We can see here how Husserl turns to 'the table' as an object by looking at it rather than over it. The writing table, if we are to follow this line, would not be seen (even if we face it, it is in the background as what is more and less familiar). For Husserl, then to see the table means to lose sight of its function" is from Sara Ahmed's *Queer Phenomenology*.

The book Kelley brings to war is by Rainer Maria Rilke. It includes the poem about which Inger Christensen (trans. Susanna Nied) wrote, "We can ask, then, if it's possible to learn to be 'exposed on the mountains of the heart.' Isn't that just something we are, something we're born into, a destiny that we take on because we can't do anything else, or because there isn't anything else we can do?"

"Just a perfect day / You made me forget myself / I thought I was / Someone else, someone good" is from Lou Reed's "Perfect Day."

Corvid behavioral facts are from Dr. John Marzluff's research at the University of Washington.

The crystallized branch is from Stendhal's *On Love,* translated by Sophie Lewis.

"I hope you suffer little additional violence" is from Lise Haller Baggesen's "Letter of Reparation," which is also a letter to her daughter.

"SHINE THE LIGHT ON THE FOLKS HONEY / YOU ARE MY FRIEND MY FRIEND" is from Sylvester's cover of "You Are My Friend," written by Patti LaBelle, Armstead Edwards, and James "Budd" Ellison.

The comedian playing "I Trusted You" is Andy Kaufman.

Caterpillar and butterfly facts are from Douglas Blackiston's research at Georgetown University.

The thunderstorm with a shaggy belly is from Ted Kooser's poem "Mother."

The gorilla is in conversation with Francine Patterson.

"WELL, I NEED YOUR LOVE" is from "Your Love," by Frankie Knuckles and Jamie Principle.

"RESIST PSYCHIC DEATH" is a Bikini Kill song.

These books, in particular but not always directly, helped me write about Antigone. Many also helped me as a person:

Ahmed, Sara. *The Promise of Happiness*. Duke University Press, 2010.
---. *Willful Subjects*. Duke University Press, 2014.

Anger, Kenneth. *Hollywood Babylon*. Jean-Jacques Pauvert, 1959.

Bachelard, Gaston. *The Poetics of Space*. trans. Maria Jolas. Beacon Press, 1994.

Baldwin, James. *The Fire Next Time*. Vintage, 1992.

Beckett, Samuel and James Knowlson. *The Theatrical Notebooks of Samuel Beckett: Krapp's Last Tape*. Faber and Faber, 1993.

Belcourt, Billy-Ray. *A History of My Brief Body*. Two Dollar Radio, 2020.

Berlant, Lauren. *Cruel Optimism*. Duke University Press, 2011.
---. *The Queen of America Goes to Washington City: Essays on Sex and Citizenship*. Duke University Press, 1997.
---, ed. *Compassion: The Culture and Politics of an Emotion*. Routledge, 2004.

Bernanos, Georges. *Mouchette*. trans. J.C. Whitehouse. New York Review Books Classics, 2005.

binaohan, b. *decolonizing trans/gender 101*. biyuti publishing, 2014.

Block, Francesca Lia. *Weetzie Bat*. HarperCollins, 1989.

Brown, Adrienne Maree. "What is/isn't transformative justice?" 2015.

Browne, Simone. *Dark Matters: On the Surveillance of Blackness*. Duke University Press, 2015.

Bouissac, Paul. *The Semiotics of Clowns and Clowning: Rituals of Transgression and the Theory of Laughter*. Bloomsbury, 2015.

Boyer, Anne. *The Undying*. Farrar, Straus and Giroux, 2019.

Butler, Judith. *Antigone's Claim*. Columbia University Press, 2000.
---. *Undoing Gender*. Routledge, 2004.

Butler, Octavia. *Parable of the Sower*. Grand Central Publishing, 2000.

Chanter, Tina. *Whose Antigone? The Tragic Marginalization of Slavery*. SUNY Press, 2011.

Chanter, Tina and Sean D. Kirkland, eds. *The Returns of Antigone*. SUNY Press, 2015.

Clare, Eli. *Brilliant Imperfection*. Duke University Press, 2017.

Clift, Sarah. *Committing the Future to Memory: History, Experience, Trauma*. Fordham University Press, 2013.

Cvetkovich, Ann. *An Archive of Feelings*. Duke University Press, 2003.
---. *Depression: A Public Feeling*. Duke University Press, 2012.

Davis, Angela. *An Autobiography*. Random House, 1974.

Debord, Guy. *Society of the Spectacle*. trans. Ken Knabb. AK Press, 2005.

Dixon, Ejeris, and Leah Lakshmi Piepzna-Samarasinha. *Beyond Survival: Strategies and Stories from the Transformative Justice Movement*. AK Press, 2020.

Edelman, Lee. *No Future: Queer Theory and the Death Drive*. Duke University Press, 2004.

Fake, Edie. *Gaylord Phoenix*. Printed Matter, 2010.
---. *Memory Palaces*. Secret Acres, 2014.

Freeman, Marilyn. *The Illuminated Space: A Personal Theory and Contemplative Practice of Media Art*. The 3rd Thing, 2020.

Gladman, Renée. *Ana Patova Crosses a Bridge*. Dorothy Project, 2013.
---. *To After That (TOAF)*. Ateleos, 2008.

Glück, Robert. *Margery Kempe*. High Risk Books, 1994.

Glück, Robert, Mary Burger, Camille Roy, and Gail Scott, eds. *Biting the Error: Writers Explore Narrative*. Coach House, 2004.

Goldin, Nan. *The Ballad of Sexual Dependency*. Aperture Press, 2005.

Gordon, Avery F. *Ghostly Matters: Haunting and the Sociological Imagination*. University of Minnesota Press, 2008.

Gornick, Vivian. *The End of the Novel of Love*. Beacon Press, 1997.

Goulish, Matthew. *39 Microlectures: in Proximity of Performance*. Routledge, 2000.

Haraway, Donna J. *Staying with the Trouble: Making Kin in the Chthulucene*. Duke University Press, 2016.

Hartman, Saidiya. "Venus in Two Acts." *Small Axe*. Duke University Press, 2008.

Hilsum, Lindsey. *In Extremis: The Life and Death of the War Correspondent Marie Colvin*. Farrar, Straus and Giroux, 2018.

Holland, Sharon Patricia. *Raising the Dead*. Duke University Press, 2000.

Howe, Fanny. *The Wedding Dress: Meditations on Word and Life*. University of California Press, 2003.

Howe, Susan. *The Birth-mark*. Wesleyan University Press, 1993.

Jung, Carl and Aniela Jaffe. *Memories, Dreams, Reflections.* trans. Clara Winston and Richard Winston. Vintage, 1989.

Kane, Sarah. *Complete Plays*. Bloomsbury, 2001.

Kimmerer, Robin Wall. *Gathering Moss*. Oregon State University Press, 2003.
---. *Braiding Sweetgrass*. Milkweed Editions, 2013.

Kitto, H.D.F. *Greek Tragedy*. Routledge, 2011.

L'Engle, Madeleine. *A Wrinkle in Time.* Ariel Books, 1962.

Levine, Stacey. *Frances Johnson*. Verse Chorus Press, 2010.

Lispector, Clarice. *Àgua Viva.* trans. Stefan Tobler. New Directions, 2012.

Macy, Joanna R. *Despair and Personal Power in the Nuclear Age.* New Society Publishers, 1983.

Malloch, Stephen and Colwyn Trevarthen. *Communicative Musicality: Exploring the Basis of Human Companionship.* Oxford University Press, 2010.

Milstein, Cindy, ed. *Rebellious Mourning: The Collective Work of Grief.* AK Press, 2017.

Muñoz, Jose Ésteban. *Cruising Utopia: The Then and There of Queer Futurity*. New York University Press, 2009.

Newton, Huey. *To Die for the People*. Reissue. City Lights, 2009.

Ngai, Sianne. *Ugly Feelings*. Harvard University Press, 2007.

Notley, Alice. *The Descent of Alette*. Penguin, 1996.

---. *Alma, or, The Dead Women*. Granary Books, 2006.

okpik, dg nanouk. *corpse whale*. University of Arizona Press, 2012.

Oliver, Akilah. *A Toast in the House of Friends*. Coffee House Press, 2009.

Oliveros, Pauline. *Deep Listening: A Composer's Sound Practice*. iUniverse, 2005.

Schneider, Rebecca. *Performing Remains: Art and War in Times of Theatrical Reenactment*. Routledge, 2011.

Schulman, Sarah. *Conflict Is Not Abuse*. Arsenal Pulp Press, 2016.

---. *The Cosmopolitans*. Feminist Press, 2016.

Sedgwick, Eve Kosofsky. *Touching Feeling: Affect, Pedagogy, Performativity*. Duke University Press, 2003.

Shakur, Assata. *Assata: An Autobiography*. Lawrence Hill Press, 2001.

Sharpe, Christina. *In the Wake: On Blackness and Being*. Duke University Press, 2016.

Sophocles. *Antigone*. trans. Jean Anouilh. Hill and Wang, 1990.
---. *Antigone*. trans. Bertolt Brecht, trans. Friedrich Holderlin and Judith Malina. Applause Theatre and Cinema Books, 2000.
---. *Antigonick*. trans. Anne Carson. New Directions, 2012.
---. *The Burial at Thebes*. trans. Seamus Heaney. Farrar, Straus and Giroux, 2005.
---. *The Three Theban Plays*. trans. Robert Fagles. Penguin, 2000.

Spade, Dean. *Normal Life: Administrative Violence, Critical Trans Politics, and the Limits of Law*. Duke University Press, 2015.

Spahr, Juliana. *Everybody's Autonomy: Connective Reading and Collective Identity*. University of Alabama Press, 2001.

Spahr, Juliana and David Buuck. *An Army of Lovers*. City Lights, 2013.

Stewart, Susan. *On Longing: Narratives of the Miniature, the Gigantic, the Souvenir, the Collection*. Duke University Press, 1992.

Stryker, Susan. "My Words to Victor Frankenstein Above the Village of Chamounix: Performing Transgender Rage." *A Journal of Lesbian and Gay Studies*, 1994.

Sycamore, Mattilda Bernstein. *The Freezer Door.* Semiotext(e), 2020.

Uribe, Sara. *Antígonia González.* trans. John Pluecker. Les Figues, 2016.

van der Kolk, Bessel. *The Body Keeps the Score: Brain, Mind, and Body in the Healing of Trauma.* Penguin, 2014.

van Hooff, Anton J. L. *From Autothanasia to Suicide: Self-Killing in Classical Antiquity.* Routledge, 2011.

Waldman, Anne. *The Iovis Trilogy: Colors in the Mechanism of Concealment.* Coffee House Press, 2011.
---. *Voice's Daughter of a Heart Yet to Be Born.* Coffee House Press, 2016.

Weems, Carrie Mae. *Past Tense.* 2016.

Weil, Simone. *Gravity and Grace.* trans. Emma Craufurd. Routledge, 2002.
---. *The Need for Roots: Prelude to a Declaration of Duties Towards Mankind.* Routledge, 2001.

Williams, Howard and Mclanie Giles. *Archaeologists and the Dead.* Oxford University Press, 2016.

Wojnarowicz, David. *Close to the Knives: A Memoir of Disintegration.* Random House, 1991.

ACKNOWLEDGMENTS

Thank you to all the people and places who helped me write about Antigone, starting with Gretchen Orsland and Gretchen Reydams-Schils. Thank you Dana DeGiulio for always talking about it. Thank you English Department at the University of Denver, especially Laird Hunt, Tayana Hardin, Selah Saterstrom, W. Scott Howard, Donna Beth Ellard, Eleni Sikelianos, Eleanor McNees, and Bin Ramke. Thank you colleagues and friends at the Naropa Summer Writing Program and Kerouac School of Disembodied Poetics. Thank you Liz Acosta for practice. Thank you yoga teachers. Thank you ACRE, the Wassaic Project, the Public Media Institute, and Joong Boo Residency for time, space, and community. Thank you Rosa Samuelson for caring so much. Thank you Sarah Schantz for the fence to write orange. Thank you front window corners at Forest Room 5 and My Brother's Bar. Thank you second floor futon at the Nightingale. Thank you Hideout. Thank you Pop Con. Thank you Wildings and Tart Parlor.

Thank you Sammi Skolmoski, you truly elegant professional, and Erika Hodges for the walk home. Thank you Jason Sommer and Sam Axelrod. Thank you Zach Dodson for your eye, timing, and friendship.

Thank you for the conversations and being-with that anchored *Tiny* (and me): Stephanie Acosta, Swanee Astrid, Mona Awad,

Katie Beavan, Drew Bouchard, Jerry Boyle, Kevin Bozelka, Amy Brauer, Joel Calahan, Mariapaz Camargo, Teresa Carmody, Toby Carroll, Adi Celt, Salem Collo-Julin, Tom Comerford, Hannah Conlon, Jessa Crispin, Emily Culliton, Tine DeFiore, Joshua Dumas, Natalie Earnhart, Kaia Fischer, Marc Fischer, Lee Hunts, Gretchen Kalwinski, Amy Karnaze, Rob Leitzell, Christy LeMaster, Jeanne Liotta, Janice Lowe, Matt Malooly, Edward Marszewski, Michaelangelo Matos, Sarah McCarry, Kristi McGuire, Chloe McLaren, Chris O'Leary, Ruth Oppenheim-Rothschild, Lisa Jane Persky, Maggie Queeney, Curtis Romero, Caryn Rose, Fred Sasaki, Taryn Schwilling, Kelly Sears, Eric Siegel, Ezra Stone, Nell Taylor, Cait Turner, Garen Whitmore, Aunt Shannon, and the whole entire Emmett Otter Family.

Thank you to my parents, Kevin and Mary. Thank you to my sister and brother, Siobhan Case and Tafadzwa Muguwe. Hello Ronan! I love you.

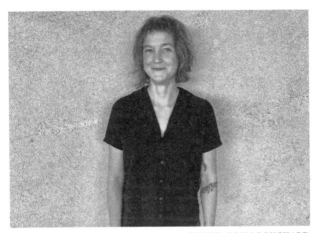

PHOTO: DREW BOUCHARD

Mairead Case is a working writer born in 1983.

R
E
S
I
S
T

P
S
Y
C
H
I
C

D
E
A
T
H